"Why did the chief of police send you over here to be my bodyguard?" Amber asked.

Garrett realized she'd read him too well. "I know you saw something in that parking lot, Amber. And the chief knows you saw something, but..."

"But what?"

"Nothing has turned up. They found no evidence of any kind of struggle like you described."

Amber turned and walked to the door. "Please go now. I don't have time for this."

"Wait! They believe you. *I* believe you. It's just that there's still nothing more to go on. The chief hoped I could talk through it with you again, maybe find a lead...."

Amber looked skeptical. "I've told you everything I know. I've been in to try to talk to the police every day...they've never asked any more questions. No one is willing to even talk to me, Garrett."

"Give me a chance to figure this out, Amber, before the suspect can target you, too. I'm not giving up on this case until I have answers."

Books by Carol Steward

Love Inspired Suspense

*Guardian of Justice
In His Sights
*Badge of Honor
*Shield of Refuge

*In the Line of Fire

Love Inspired

There Comes a Season   This Time Forever
Her Kind of Hero   Finding Amy
Second Time Around   Finding Her Home
Courting Katarina   Journey to Forever

CAROL STEWARD

To Carol Steward, selling a book is much like riding a roller coaster—every step of the process, every sale brings that exhilarating high. During the less exciting times, she's busy gathering ideas and refilling her cup. Writing brings a much needed balance to her life, as she has her character share lessons she herself learned.

When she's not working at the University of Northern Colorado, you can usually find her spending time with her husband of more than thirty years, writing and thanking God she survived raising her own three children to reap His rewards of playing with her adorable grandchildren.

Throughout all of the different seasons of life, God has continued to teach Carol to turn to Him. She has also learned to simplify her life and appreciate her many blessings—His gift of creativity, sharing her love for God with readers and setting an example of what God can do when we say, "Yes, God, take me, shape me, use me." To find out more about Carol's slightly crazy life and her books, visit her Web site at www.carolsteward.com.

SHIELD *of* REFUGE

Carol Steward

Steeple
Hill®

Published by Steeple Hill Books™

STEEPLE HILL BOOKS

Steeple
Hill®

ISBN-13: 978-0-373-44315-4
ISBN-10: 0-373-44315-3

SHIELD OF REFUGE

Printed in U.S.A.

This God, His way is perfect; the promise of the Lord proves true; He is a shield for all those who take refuge in Him.

—*2 Samuel* 22:31

There are so many people who have helped me through this book and who have inspired this story, there's no way to list everyone. My editor, Melissa, for your patience, my family for taking care of me for a change, to my friends for understanding and holding me up in prayer and to my precious granddaughter and grandson, Grandma is ready to play!

And to my son, Scott, and the love of his life, God has a plan, hold on to His promise.

ONE

Amber Scott rushed into the Victorian Inn with the bottom tier of the anniversary cake. The other layers and tools were already inside and prepped for assembly. She only had a few minutes to put this cake together and get the other one to her friend's wedding shower across town.

Thanks to her assistant going home sick midafternoon, Amber was running behind on everything. She'd had several last-minute customers looking for just the right costume for the harvest party at the senior center. Her grandmother's friends were thrilled with the changes Amber had made to Nana's bakery and with her determination to keep the business alive.

She squeezed the bag of icing, piping the finishing touches to the bottom layer, then placed the six-inch heart layer on top of the base cake and piped a reverse-scroll design to cover the seam between the two cakes. After a final inspection, Amber left the invoice with the headwaiter and rushed out to her van.

A white car with a portable police beacon on top—like those she'd seen on reruns of T.V. cop shows—

had pulled up behind the parked cars. The odd thing was, the beacon wasn't lit.

In a hurry to get to her friend's wedding shower, Amber pressed the sliding-door opener on the key fob, set her decorating kit into the gap, and rearranged the boxes of supplies and favors so the shower cake wouldn't slide around and get damaged.

After a quick study of the officer's haphazard parking job, Amber determined it was parked too close for her to back out. Her breathing quickened as she thought of asking him to move a little.

She didn't like cops.

Just wait patiently until he's gone.

She grabbed the gift bag for the shower and set it on the passenger's seat and glanced at the policeman as he talked to the driver of a yellow SUV. He nodded toward his car, then grabbed the car door and yanked it open.

Amber felt a sudden chill.

The cop pulled the driver out of the vehicle. She looked young and pretty…and vulnerable.

Amber heard the woman protest, though she wasn't exactly sure what she'd said. Watching the confrontation through the tinted windows, Amber wondered if the two knew each other.

The officer looked as if he was whispering in her ear, and Amber began to believe it was true.

Suddenly he grabbed her arm and pulled her to the unmarked car and the woman struggled to get away. She was wearing athletic pants and one of those tight-fitting tops with a hood that she'd seen the volleyball players wear into the shop. The door of the yellow SUV stood wide open.

Amber's heart raced as the officer struggled to get the cuffs on the girl. She jumped into the driver's seat, closed and locked the doors, trying to avoid bringing any attention to herself.

She searched for her cell phone. Not finding it on the console, she reached for her purse, hoping she'd dropped it in there. Her eyes darted nervously from the purse to the confrontation outside.

They must know each other. If not, why wasn't she yelling? Or running? Something was wrong.

The girl freed one arm and took a swing at him. He lunged back, and the two rolled against the car as he fought to pull her other arm back into the cuffs. The struggle untucked his uniform shirt and the fabric billowed in the cold breeze. She screamed, and he snapped his hand over her mouth, pressing something into the small of her back. The handcuffed woman arched her back, then went limp. He gave her a final shove into the car, pushed her feet inside and closed the door. He hurried to the other side, stumbling at the trunk.

Amber was stunned. Was he a real officer? She tried to ward away the sick feeling in her stomach. If he was a real officer, she would be crazy to confront him. Not with her past. She had just put her problems behind her. She didn't need to dig up trouble now.

While history told her to mind her own business, the new faith she'd found in God told her this wasn't what it looked like. *God, what should I do?*

She quickly replayed the incident in her mind. She realized she'd never seen an officer cover someone's mouth. He was crazy to use a bare hand. His uniform looked like those on the costume racks in her shop: baggy enough to fit any build, light, flimsy fabric to go over a coat or sweatshirt. And he didn't have a gun belt or radio, or any of the official-looking things Amber remembered from when police visited the dorms.

Her heart seemed to be following her racing brain, trying to keep pace. She was breathing fast. She looked over her shoulder as the police officer pulled the bubble light into the car and sped away.

Be with that girl, God. Protect her....

After several encounters with the police in her freshman year, she really didn't like talking to the police. She had to call. But what would she say? If it was police brutality, would they even believe her, or would they accuse her of false reporting? Were the underage drinking charges, fake ID and running from the police still on her record?

Just call, before it's too late, she told herself. She found her phone, dialed 911 and pressed the send button before she chickened out again.

I can't let this happen. I can stop him from hurting her.

She backed out of the diagonal parking space trying to juggle her phone and shift gears, hoping she could find the car and help the woman. She glanced around. Not seeing it, she pressed the speaker phone.

"911 operator, what's your emergency?"

"I'm outside the Victorian Inn just off the University Campus. I just saw a police officer push a woman into an unmarked car. Only I don't think he's really an officer."

The woman didn't respond, and Amber wondered if they'd been disconnected. "Did you hear me?"

"Yes, I'm sending an officer to check it out," the woman said, slightly rattled. "Are you okay?"

"I'm fine. I don't think he saw me."

Her mind was playing games with her. Like the e-mail she'd received this afternoon with the geometric designs. The designs had been spinning like a pinwheel in a tornado, which was supposedly a sign of intense stress. The design hadn't been moving at all.

She had blown off the psychological analysis of the e-mail as nothing more than an optical illusion.

Now here she was witnessing a crime and calling the cops. Seeing a police officer pushing a woman into an unmarked car just wasn't right. The police were going to think she'd lost her mind. Right now, she would agree.

She started to hang up, then thought again about the girl.

Of course she was right to call the police. She'd already missed her chance to stop the assault. Maybe it wasn't too late….

"What is your current location?" The operator pulled Amber's attention back to the bizarre events that she'd just witnessed.

"I'm at—" she had to rethink her delivery instructions "—The Victorian Inn is on University and…Elm. I delivered a cake there," she started to explain before realizing that wasn't important. "The crime happened there, now the car is a few blocks ahead of me. He turned on Maple." She pressed on the gas. "When I came out…of the inn, I mean… I heard a man ordering a young woman to get out of her car. They struggled, and then she just went limp and he stuffed her into the backseat and took off."

"Your name?"

"Amber…" Her past mistakes haunted her. It was too late to back away now. She took off after the car. "Did you hear what I said?"

"Yes, Amber, I'm sending officers to talk to you."

"He's turned again. He's heading north on…just a minute, here comes a street sign."

"He's moving?" the operator squeaked, forcing calm to her voice. "Are you following him?"

"Yes, I told you, he drove away, with the girl…" Amber said, struggling with whether to speed up and catch them, or keep her distance. If she caught up to them, what then?

"Amber, did you get a license number before he took off?"

She pressed the gas. "Other than it was from here in Colorado, no, but I could catch up to him. Are you saying he really wasn't an officer?"

"We're still trying to determine that. I've dispatched any available units. Give me your current location, then pull to the side of the road and stop."

"He just turned left on…Cherry Pit Avenue."

Amber had already entered the intersection. She slowed down to make the turn. "Where'd he go?"

She glanced right and left searching for him. Sirens warbled from all directions. They'd probably scared him. Where could he have disappeared to in a residential area like this? She searched for open garages or alleys where he could have hidden.

The sirens were getting louder. She looked up just in time to see a silver vehicle cross in front of her. She slammed on the brakes and straightened her arms, pressing her hands into the steering wheel as she heard the crunch and scrape of her van hitting the back fender.

The SUV spun in slow motion, police lights flashing, sirens screeching. Then the silver vehicle tipped up on two wheels, flipped over to its roof and twirled like a top.

Amber screamed as her van fishtailed before coming to a stop at the opposite curb. "Oh, no…. I hit him! Oh, no. Oh, no. Oh, please let him be okay. Let him be okay, please. Help! 911, send help, fast!"

TWO

The woman who had hit him jumped out of her van and ran toward his police cruiser. He smelled fumes, turned and saw gasoline flowing toward him.

Hanging upside down from the seatbelt, Garrett Matthews looked out the window to see a woman's legs in black tights and black suede fashion boots. She kicked the shards of glass aside with her boots, then dropped to the ground, a black-and-turquoise patterned dress floating over her knees.

"You've got to get out. There's gas gushing out all over," she said frantically.

He glanced at her, disoriented, then pressed the button on the mike. "Dispatch, Officer four-six-three involved in two-car rollover accident at intersection of—" he glanced around "—where are we?" he said to the woman.

"Just get out of there!" she yelled. "I'm still on with 911, they're sending help." She took a deep breath and coughed from the fumes. "Come on, we need to get you out."

He turned the key to off and removed it, handing it

to the woman for safekeeping. She looked at it oddly, furrowing her brows.

What was he thinking?

Tugging on the seat belt strapping him upside down, Garrett struggled with the buckle to release. "It's jammed." He reached for the glove box, hoping to find an emergency kit. It was out of his reach. His knife was in his belt, securely trapped under the seat belt. "I need something sharp."

"Just a minute." She ran to the van and returned with a ten-inch serrated knife. The woman was gorgeous. She dropped to her knees and reached inside, directing the knife to the gray strap stretched across his chest.

His eyes opened wide and suddenly the fog lifted from his mind. "Aren't you in enough trouble without threatening an officer? Give me that."

"What?" She backed away. "I'm trying to save your life. I don't mean to panic you, but gas is spilling—the car may blow up."

"The car's not going to blow up," he insisted. "May I borrow your knife?" She hesitated, then handed it to him. He took the handle, and with a sawing motion he cut through the mesh strap and fell to the ground, landing on his head. "Why are you carrying a knife around in your car?"

"I'm a cake decorator. It's in my delivery kit. Come on, you have to get out."

He twisted his wide shoulders, shoving the objects that had scattered across the roof out of the way while reaching for the window opening. He looked up to her huge blue eyes as he tried to find something to push against. "I don't suppose this door will open, will it? When I pull on the latch, you pull on the door."

The woman found a place with no glass and tugged as he pushed. "I don't think so. Do you want me to try the other side?"

"No, I'll get out somehow."

"Let me get the glass out of the way so you don't cut yourself." She kicked at the tiny pellets of glass with her boot.

"Don't bother," he growled, then, realizing she was right—he just needed to get out. If they had to pull glass from his back, so be it. The fumes were making him sick. He waved her aside and used his legs to push himself out the narrow window, all the time trying to ignore the Marilyn Monroe look-alike waiting for him.

"Come on!" She tapped her boot, holding the billowy skirt of her dress against her legs as he pulled his ticket can from the cruiser and collected a few more belongings. She pulled on his arm as he stumbled to his feet and picked up his ticket can. "Are you okay? Maybe you should sit down."

With a healthy tan and shimmering brownish-blond tendrils of hair softening the dramatic high cheekbones and narrow nose, she was gorgeous. How could he be angry with that look of concern in her brilliant blue eyes?

He shrugged, sending a pain down his arm. He needed to ignore the niggling reminder that he should have slowed down at each intersection. Much as he wanted to blame her, and her alone, he couldn't. He needed to get on with his job. He looked around, assessing the situation, then started to radio in their location.

"I'm so sorry. I wanted to find that car and get the license plate number…."

He took his hand off the mike. "You're the reporting party? You're Amber?"

She looked terrified, but nodded.

He reached for his notepad and pen in his chest pocket, realizing too late that they'd fallen out when he turned over in the SUV. "They didn't give your last name." He opened the lid of the clipboard and pulled out a ticket and pen.

"Amber Scott," she said softly. She backed away. "I was afraid to try to stop him. I could've at least yelled…I should have backed my van into him, but I just had it painted…." She looked at it and shook her head. "Lot of good that did—look at it now."

Paintings of bright-colored balloons and streamers were crumpled and smooshed all over the front fender of the minivan. "It's just a machine. It can be repaired." His head started spinning. His shoulder burned. "You did the right thing not getting involved. If you had tried to intervene there may have been two women apprehended. Only thing you shouldn't have done was follow him. How're you doing? Are you hurt?"

"No, I'm fine."

He gave her another once over, concurring with her assessment. She looked mighty fine. He forced himself to process the accident as if he weren't a victim. If he focused on the scene, maybe he wouldn't hurt so bad. "We'll let the paramedics check you out just as a precaution." He looked at his police cruiser and shook his head. So much for his perfect record.

"They really don't need to do that. I'm so sorry about the accident. Are you okay?"

"I'm sure it's nothing serious," he said, hoping that saying it would make it so. "So what kind of car was it?"

"What kind of car?" Amber stared at him and shrugged. "I don't know. It looked like a police car except it was white and didn't have the logo and police stripes."

"A Crown Vic?"

"A what?"

"Crown Victoria…that's the model of car used by the police around here. Huge boat, like your grandparents probably drove back in the seventies."

"Sure," she said with a blank stare.

He took hold of her arm and pulled her away from the overturned vehicle as she rattled off details he wasn't going to be able to remember, let alone make any sense of.

"A woman was forced into the backseat."

"A four-door sedan, then," he said, stopping just inches from her.

"Yeah," she said. "I was trying to help, but…" She backed away from him and crossed her arms across her chest. "They're still looking for the car, right?" Sirens came to a stop as more officers arrived, surrounding them.

"Oh, no, I hit a cop," she mumbled. She paced frantically, hugging her arms to her body.

"That's just dawning on you?" He could almost

feel her pain. She stared at him, her blue eyes framed with long lashes.

"Well, no…but…I think it's just sinking in. Really sinking in, I mean." She had a sick look on her face. "I'm so sorry. I was trying to find the car. It looked like he killed her."

"You didn't tell that to dispatch."

She stopped pacing. "Didn't I?" she asked, looking him in the eye. She sidestepped away from the two officers who were headed their way.

"You okay?" each officer echoed as they approached.

Amber didn't respond.

"Yeah, we're doing okay," Garrett answered. Despite his claim, the officers radioed for an ambulance and tow trucks, then dispersed to assess the damage.

He turned back to Ms. Scott, staggering slightly. "So what makes you think he killed her?" he asked, trying to keep his balance. He couldn't believe this had happened. What rotten timing. He had been in perfect health when he'd applied to the federal agencies. Becoming a fed had always been his dream. Now that he had a year of street patrol experience under his belt and his master's degree, he'd been sure he'd get a call. Until now. Perfect health, perfect record—all gone in an instant.

"The woman was fighting against him, then she just went limp. Like she'd just dropped dead. There was no noise, nothing."

Garrett studied the woman who'd run into him, trying to ignore her brilliant blue eyes—eyes that couldn't tell a lie if she tried. He'd bet his life on it. "Did you see anything else? Blood? A knife? A gun?" He didn't want to embarrass her by pointing out that a body went limp when someone fainted, too. Feeling a little light-headed himself, Garrett felt himself sway.

Before the woman could answer, Lieutenant Chavez ordered him to sit down. "An ambulance is on the way, Matthews." As Garrett looked for a place to collapse, the lieutenant addressed the woman who'd ruined his record. "Are you okay?"

"Yes, I'm fine," she insisted, pushing past the lieutenant and the other officer and closer to Garrett. "I didn't see any blood. I was looking through the tinted glass, so it was too dark, and…" She paused. "I couldn't see whether it was a knife, or gun, but I didn't hear a gunshot."

"This is our RP, Lieutenant. Amber Scott. She was following the suspect…" The flashing lights of the squad cars were making him sick. "Could you ask them to turn off the flashers?"

While another officer went to give the order, Amber started explaining why she'd been following.

"Did you find the girl? The car?" she asked before she explained, again, what she had witnessed.

Lieutenant Chavez brushed her concerns aside, suggesting she needed to calm down and wait for the ambulance to arrive. "We'll handle…"

She lifted her hand to her hip. "You're not listening to me," Amber insisted, clearly annoyed with technicalities of anything but the crime. "She was trying to scream and he covered her mouth with his hand, then suddenly she went limp." Another officer approached and tried to lead her away. "But what about the girl? The car? Why are you all here, and not looking for her?"

"Don't worry, Ms...." Garrett said, trying to ignore the dizziness. He glanced at his fellow officer.

Lieutenant Chavez shone his flashlight in Garrett's face. "Garrett? You okay?"

He didn't answer.

Amber turned and looked at him. She pressed her key fob, opening the sliding door of her van behind her. "Here," she said. "Sit down while you wait for the ambulance. Just watch out for the cake box." She re-arranged things, then slid the box to the back of the van. "Oh, no, the shower. I'm going to be late. I need to make a phone call."

"I'm afraid you're going to be more than late, Ms. Scott. Make your call," Lieutenant Chavez said, then looked at him. "Sit down, Garrett."

He was in no condition to ignore an order. He sat in the doorway and took a deep breath, inhaling the sweet, nauseating aroma of a bakery mixed with gas fumes.

God, don't let this be serious. He fought off the nausea, eyeing the interesting mess inside—plastic umbrellas, a gift bag with satin spaghetti straps dangling from the front seat, and a small box of what he hoped had nothing to do with the rest of her assortment. He had to be seeing things.

She must have seen his reaction to the contents, as she reached past him and tucked the flimsy fabric into a gift bag and apologized for the mess. "I was making deliveries on the way to a friend's wedding shower... when I saw the officer..."

"Officer? What kind of officer?" Chavez asked as he approached.

"Police," she whispered, looking more terrified by the minute. "It was a police costume, I think. The more I've thought about it, I don't think it was real. The fabric was too thin and blew when she ripped it from his pants. It wasn't made as well as yours." She stole a glance at Garrett's shirt. "Are you wearing a bulletproof vest?"

"Excuse me?"

"Well, I noticed that the policeman's shirt, the impersonator policeman…" she stammered, "his was too baggy, but it didn't register until now. It's probably because you all wear bulletproof vests, right?"

If Garrett hadn't felt like throwing up, he'd have laughed.

"Yeah, what else did you notice?" the lieutenant asked, skepticism dripping from each word.

"He covered her mouth with his hand. I've never seen any real officer doing that…." She looked nervously from Chavez back to Garrett. "Especially with a bare hand. I mean, some drug addict could bite you, right?" Her fear-filled eyes met Garrett's again as a state patrol officer arrived and introduced himself.

Garrett wondered if she'd be half as gorgeous if he hadn't hit his head. While a couple officers were cleaning up the gasoline with kitty litter, the others were simply staring at Amber Scott. Apparently her good looks weren't his imagination. Her blond hair was pulled back into a clip and looked like she'd knocked the clip askew in the accident.

He glanced back at the shower gift and cake as the

state patrolman walked around the van, inspecting the scene with a raised eyebrow. "Interesting cargo, Ms. Scott," the patrolman said, vocalizing Garrett's thoughts. He pulled his ticket book from the metal clipboard. "May I have your license and registration, please?"

She had to get into the van in order to find the documents, then dug through her purse for her driver's license. "Have they found the car yet?"

"I'm mainly concerned with Officer Matthews's and your safety right now," the state patrolman replied with a cocky smile. "Have you had anything to drink this evening?"

"No," she answered, then turned back to her glove box.

The patrolman ran his gaze up and down Amber, then gave her a look of contempt. "Would you agree to a test?"

Garrett didn't like the way he was eyeing her.

She propped her forearm on the steering wheel. "That's fine, I don't drink, and I don't do drugs. I was…"

Garrett intervened. "Colorado State Patrol is only here to process the accident," he said, "because Fossil Creek Police Department can't investigate our own accidents."

Amber slid out of the van and handed everything to the patrolman while one of the officers was measuring the skid marks and taking pictures of the vehicles, inside and out.

The patrolman glared at Garrett, then turned to talk to the lieutenant. The two moved to look under the van, probably to verify how much fluid it had lost, he thought.

She closed the front door, then leaned against the van next to Garrett. "What if it's the rapist that everyone's been looking for?"

"We already caught him, and this wasn't the same MO," Garrett muttered before the lieutenant heard and got involved again.

"Oh, I guess I missed that in the newspaper." She began to wring her hands. "But this girl could be hurt."

"It's okay, calm down—just answer the officer's questions. Don't offer more," Garrett mumbled.

Amber leaned closer and whispered to him. "Are the charges for hitting a cop worse than running into someone else?"

"Not unless I mention the knife," he said with a wink.

"That's not funny," she said, a nervous smile twitching her lip. "I was only trying to help."

His gaze met hers and they both smiled. "No, hitting a cop is no different, unless it's intentional." He glanced at the geometric designs on her dress, then back to her alluring face. He'd never reacted this way to anyone on the job.

"Well, if one judged by the dozen or so glowering stares I'm receiving from them, one would think so. Can't some of these officers go looking for the girl? He's getting away."

"He's already gotten away," Garrett said as he closed his eyes and rested his head in his hands. "Don't be concerned about the officers. They…" *They're trying not to drool.* The image brought a brief mental smile. "Don't worry, the Fossil Creek Police Department will ask you about the crime you witnessed after the accident is processed," he said quietly, hoping he didn't sound as bad as he felt. *I just wish you hadn't hit me.* He inhaled a breath of fresh air, propping his knees on his elbows.

"What's your name? Garrett or Matthew? I heard them call you both. I want to be praying that your injuries aren't serious. If that's okay, I mean. I guess God knows who I hit, but it would mean more to me to know I'm praying for you personally. I owe you at least that much."

"Garrett Matthews. I can use all the prayers I can get. Thanks."

"They don't believe me, do they?"

"They'll look into it," he mumbled, not wanting to admit there were far too many officers standing here, gawking like the civilians they made fun of for chasing emergency lights. They shouldn't be here, but that wasn't his call. He had just finished his rookie year.

A compact car drove up and parked nearby. Another woman approached one of the officers, then spotted Amber and made a beeline for her. "Are you okay?" Guessing by the hug, Garrett figured she was the friend hosting the shower.

"Yeah, I'm okay, but I'm not sure about the officer I hit. I'll call you later." Her voice got softer as she spoke. Amber carried the cake and the gift to the car. "Don't mention my accident to Maya. No need to panic the bride two weeks before the wedding. I'll figure out a way to get the cake to the resort. I don't need her to worry about that, too—"

The state patrolman interrupted. "Your van's going to be in the shop for a while, so if you need any of the other things, you may as well send them with your friend now."

The women quickly moved everything from van to car and the friend left.

When Amber returned to the empty van, Garrett smiled. "Handcuffs for a wedding shower?"

"Handcuffs? Oh, no, those aren't for the shower." Her porcelain skin turned bright pink. "Parties Galore also has costumes and decorations. I was going to re-package them for costume parties. They were on back order and just came in. Police costumes are very popular, you know."

"I see. Bride's name wouldn't happen to be Sarah, would it?"

"I'm afraid I can't share my client's information." She quirked her eyebrow, trying to hide her smile. "Why? Is that your fiancée?"

"My *what?*" He laughed. "No way." Garrett shook his head. "Future sister-in-law," he whispered.

"Well, send her my way. I'm a party planner and owner of Parties Galore—used to be the bakery downtown. Weddings are my specialty."

"I see." He forced a smile as he stood. Flashing lights caught his attention and he headed toward the ambulance. "I'll be sure to pass along your name."

She studied him. "Are you okay? You look kind of pale. Maybe you need some food. I should have offered you a bite of cake."

"No," he growled. "I'm not much for sweets, even when I'm feeling good."

Just as he started to weave, Amber stepped up next

to him and wrapped her arm around his waist. "Here, lean on my shoulder," she said, then called for help. The paramedics rushed to her aid with the gurney and took his vitals, then put a neck brace on. "I don't need that. There's nothing wrong..." he argued, even though he knew it was futile.

Lieutenant Chavez reminded Garrett that it was a requirement that he get checked out in any on-duty accident.

Garrett watched the fear escalate in Amber's eyes and fought the inclination to be angry with her. While he didn't feel fine, he knew he had to do something to ease Amber Scott's guilt. It wasn't as if she'd been rushing to make it to the wedding shower. She was after a kidnapper, just as he would have been under the same circumstances.

A few minutes of oxygen in the ambulance and he'd be fine again, he was sure of it.

Garrett looked at Amber and winked. "I'm going to be fine. It's just a formality."

She didn't look convinced.

The paramedics rattled off numbers that indicated his heart was doing just fine, considering he'd just been in an accident and met an attractive woman. "Hey," he said to the lead medic. "Give me a minute, would you?" He waggled his finger, motioning for Amber to come closer.

She stepped to his side and stared at him, regret and fear washing the color from her face. "How can I ever make this right?" she asked.

"You did all the wrong things for all the right reasons. I admire you for that." He reached up and touched her hand. "That in itself is enough for me."

THREE

Amber watched in fear as they loaded the officer into the ambulance and drove away. *God, take care of Officer Matthews, and help him remember how much I regret hurting him.*

"Ms. Scott, we need to get more information from you about the crime you apparently witnessed."

"Apparently?" She knew that tone and it snapped her right out of her pity party. *Pretty blonde, just pacify her.* "I didn't 'apparently' witness anything," she said, wishing she could sound more forceful. "I *did* witness a crime, and somewhere out there a woman's life is in danger. So are you telling me you let a dozen or more officers stand here and glare at me over an innocent accident and no one was out there looking for the criminal? A police impersonator may have killed someone? That's just frightening, Officer."

"Lieutenant Chavez." He glared at her, reminding her why she disliked police officers. "If you'd have left the pursuit up to us, we wouldn't be here now, and one of my officers wouldn't be headed to the hospital."

"I can't tell you how bad I feel about Officer Matthews. I never meant for anyone to get hurt. Why else would I follow someone that had already hurt one woman?"

"I don't know, you tell me why you'd put yourself in danger when it didn't involve you? Did you recognize either of the people?" The lieutenant seemed as annoyed as Amber was.

"No. If I did, why wouldn't I tell you who it was?" She watched them load her van onto the tow truck and drive away, wondering how she was going to get home. She didn't want to ask. The lieutenant wasn't as cordial as Officer Matthews. Surely at some point they'd let her know. An officer was sweeping up the glass, but most were finally leaving, getting back onto patrol she hoped.

The officer motioned to his police cruiser. "Get in and show me where you saw the crime take place. The officers can finish up here."

Amber suddenly froze. It wasn't even intentional, though she was sure the officer wouldn't see it that way. She knew from past experience, officers didn't like their authority questioned. She certainly didn't need another resisting arrest on her record. The first time she'd been sure the plain clothes cop was an imposter, until *after* he'd caught her and cuffed her. She didn't need a repeat.

A female officer joined them. "I'm Samantha Taylor, the victim's advocate officer. Do you have someone who can pick you up after you're done tonight?"

Amber shook her head. "I'm not sure, depends on how long this takes."

"I'd guess at least another hour," Samantha said, pulling a card from her pocket.

"No, most of my friends are at a wedding shower."

"Well then, have one of the officers give me a call when you're done and I'll take you home. And here's my card."

"Thanks."

"Officer Taylor, could you come with us to the scene please?" The lieutenant gave instructions to another officer and led Amber to his squad car.

The female officer stepped into pace with them, easing Amber's concerns about being alone with the grumpy officer. The two officers sat in the front seats of the squad car and put Amber in the back.

"So, where'd this incident take place?"

She directed him to the Victorian Inn, going through the incident as he drove. After they got out, she showed him where she'd parked, and where the police car had been. "This is the yellow SUV that the woman was driving, well, not literally driving, but she was inside it. It was in this same place."

The officers took a quick look around it, using a gloved hand to try to open any of the doors. They were all locked.

"When I came out from finishing the cake, I saw the unmarked police car parked in the street behind the yellow SUV, but sort of pulled in at an angle. There, where that black Suburban is now. That's where I was parked. The cop was parked…" She looked around, pictured herself walking out of the inn, thinking about the scene. "About here." Amber pointed to the right. "There was a small car between the yellow SUV and me. The door to the SUV was open when I drove off after him, though."

"Run the plates on it, Taylor," the lieutenant ordered while he shone a flashlight both directions along the ground. "You sure this is where it happened?"

"Yes, I'm sure. I parked in the 15-minute zone because I wasn't staying much longer than to assemble a two-tier anniversary cake. This space was the only one available, because I thought it was too bad I couldn't have had the closer spot, so I wouldn't have to go around the van carrying the heavy cake. When I came out, the spot I wanted," she pointed to it, "was open. Then next to it was a red Mustang."

"I thought you told Officer Matthews you don't know cars," he said, interrupting her thought process.

"I always wanted a Mustang, so I noticed it, candy-apple red. That's when I heard the man telling her to get out of her truck. I was putting my cake kit into the van and rearranged it a little because I didn't want the cake to be damaged, since it didn't fit into a covered box. I thought of asking him to move, but I don't… I didn't have a good feeling about him."

Amber continued to explain, feeling as if she was repeating herself for nothing, while the officers both took notes and asked more questions.

Lieutenant Chavez put his flashlight back into his belt. "Did they see or hear you?"

Amber shrugged, tired of going through all of this. "Not that I'm aware of. Once I realized this wasn't really a cop, I got in the van and started looking for my phone. I was so scared. I couldn't believe what I was seeing. I keep thinking I should have honked the horn or something. I couldn't think." She felt her heart sink and tears stung her eyes. "I didn't know what to do.

Then all of a sudden, she went limp, and he forced her into the backseat of the car. And I just panicked. I couldn't believe what I'd just seen. I didn't know what to do."

"You did exactly what you should have done," the lieutenant said gently. He paused to let her compose herself before continuing the questioning. "And you have no idea if he stabbed her, or what caused her to go limp?"

"I couldn't see that well. There were shadows from the trees. It was getting dark. The guy was in the way." Amber closed her eyes and focused. "She jerked, like someone in pain. Maybe he did stab her?"

"There's no sign of a scuffle, no blood, no evidence that I can see." The female officer raised an eyebrow. "What made you think it was a police car in the first place?"

"It had one of those little bubble lights on top, like on cop shows, where they stick it up on the roof from out their window."

"We don't use any of those, even on unmarked cars," the lieutenant explained.

"I've only seen them on television, but I'm convinced that he was an imposter. I recognize the piping on the costume. I bought some of them for my shop."

"We'll need to see them, and who has rented them. And if anyone returns one, don't launder it until we've run some tests on it."

"No problem, but I haven't seen this guy in my store. The costume could have been ordered online," Amber said as the officers scoured the street for any sign of a struggle.

The lieutenant approached while the female officer

continued searching for any sign of a scuffle. "I'm going to need a physical description of each of them."

Amber thought a minute or two before confessing, "I'm not sure how much I saw. The sun was going down, and the shadows…"

After coming up with nothing, Officer Taylor said, "Stand where you were this evening." The officers both moved next to the yellow vehicle. "Is this about how tall the guy was?"

Amber compared their height to the yellow vehicle. "I think the guy was shorter than you, Lieutenant Chavez, about Officer Taylor's height, I'd guess, and the girl was about the same."

"Good," the woman said. "What else do you remember?"

"He was stocky, but not fat, a long buzz cut, and probably Hispanic. She was Caucasian, long brown or dark reddish hair maybe, for some reason, red sticks in my mind, tall, but not too thin."

"Any tattoos or jewelry on either of them?" Officer Taylor asked.

Amber shrugged, closed her eyes and tried to see the image again. "I couldn't see them that clearly."

"Any indication he might have had gang affiliations?"

She shook her head, trying to understand how someone wearing a cop uniform could also look like a gang member. "No. He was wearing a police uniform. My first impression was it was legit."

"And her?" the lieutenant asked.

"I can't be sure. She was wearing a blue tight-fitting top with a hood, but she looked like the athletes that come into my shop for their sugar fix."

"I don't see anything here. It's almost unheard of for a victim not to drop something during an abduction. I thought maybe she'd left her purse or backpack in the vehicle, but I can't be sure without getting inside. We can't do that without a warrant. Did the suspect stop for any length of time after he closed her in the police car?" Officer Taylor asked.

"It all seemed to happen so fast at the time," Amber said as she closed her eyes and walked herself through the incident again, step by step, whispering to herself.

The lieutenant took a slow walk around the area again, shaking his head.

"This doesn't seem like a sexual assault, and it definitely doesn't fit the MO of the guy we got," Officer Taylor said as she returned to Amber's side. The radio interrupted their conversation, and Samantha focused on it. "Looks like the vehicle is registered to a twenty-five-year-old male, Marcus Smith. I can check on him later."

Amber struggled to recall what the suspect looked like, relieved that Officer Taylor seemed to believe her. "Wait a minute. It's possible she had something hanging from her shoulder. She broke away once when they were almost to the car, she swung at him, and he threw her against the side of the trunk. She could have dropped something there. After he got the second cuff on her and stuffed her in the car, he stumbled when he was going around the car, but maybe he didn't stumble, maybe he stooped to pick something up."

"Are you sure about that?" the lieutenant asked.

Amber shrugged. "Pretty sure." She just realized

something she hadn't noticed before. "It was a Rocky Mountain University top. I saw it as she was being pushed into the car."

"You're sure?" he said again.

She leveled a glare at the lieutenant. She hadn't realized how comfortable she'd been answering Officer Matthews's questions. She was quickly realizing he wasn't like other cops. "I'm not making this up as I go along. I simply didn't remember every little detail before."

The female officer held out her hand. "It's normal to remember additional facts as the adrenaline wears off. Just keep writing everything down as you remember it. Someone from FCPD will be in touch if we need more information."

The lieutenant moved toward the squad car and directed them to do the same.

She was taken to the police station, where they asked her to write out her report of the incident leading up to the accident, then gave her information about contacting the towing company to schedule her transport to the repair shop. She added it to the careless driving and speeding ticket in her bag.

"Have you heard how Officer Matthews is doing?"

"No, we can't give out that information." The records clerk took the report form and turned away.

When Amber was released she assured the officer that she'd reached a friend to give her a ride. She left the station, tears stinging her eyes. She walked to the nearest bus stop, and got off at the hospital she'd overheard mentioned on the police radio. She hoped she wasn't too late to check in on Officer Matthews.

FOUR

Garrett Matthews opened his eyes and fought the nausea back with more ice chips. "The police force is already shorthanded, Doc. I can at least do something in the office, can't I?"

"The CT scan looks good, but you'll need to take a few days off from full duty, make sure this concussion is fully gone before you're back out on the streets. You're going to be pretty sore for a while."

"Nothing a few over-the-counter painkillers won't cure, right?"

"Maybe. The symptoms of whiplash very often don't show up for several days. You're not to push it. And I mean it, Garrett."

It was just his luck that their family doctor happened to be in the ER with another patient when the ambulance arrived. There was no hope of fooling Dr. Call.

"Can you arrange to have someone stay with you tonight?" the doctor asked as he wrote on Garrett's chart.

Garrett rolled his eyes and shifted on the too-short bed trying to find a comfortable position. "I'm sure you've already called Mom and Dad. And yes, they'd be happy to watch out for me."

"I couldn't reach them. Maybe one of your brothers could stay with you. I suspect Kira and her new husband might even take you in for the night if we called them."

"I'm not calling the newlyweds. Nick is working tonight, and Mom and Dad will probably be home any time. They never leave their cell phone on. Kent and Renee have gone to Mexico on vacation." Garrett felt the weight of his head smoosh the pillow.

"You rest here then until we reach someone. Headache starting?"

His eyes drifted closed. "No."

"You can't go to sleep, Garrett. And it won't do you any good to deny the headache. You're not going back to work, in any case," Dr. Call informed him. "I want to check you out in a week to clear you for full duty."

"A week?"

"Not one foot in the car, Garrett Matthews…." Dr. Call demanded as much respect now as he had when Garrett was a kid.

"But…"

"Not one. I've fought with your father when he was still on duty, and won then, too. Just because I'm old, doesn't mean you can pull a fast one over me. Your eyes are glazed over, one pupil is dilated. You have a concussion and in that condition, you're more danger to the community than you are a help. I'm going to go find a nurse or hospital volunteer to sit with you and make sure you don't fall asleep. We want to keep you awake for a while longer."

"I just want to help in the office," he said lamely as the doctor left his room.

Garrett heard a gentle knock and turned, surprised to see the woman who'd run into him walk meekly into the room.

"I just had to make sure you're okay."

He looked at her, reassured that she was just as pretty in the light. "I'm going to be fine," he said, eyeing his uniform laying across the chair. "How'd you get in here?"

She shrugged, though a pretty pink tinge colored her delicate skin. "I slipped in the exit as someone was leaving. Things get kind of hectic in an ER." She smiled softly, and Garrett felt the pain in his head ease up considerably. "The police wouldn't tell me anything. I'll leave as soon as I know you're okay, I promise. You didn't look good when they took you in the ambulance. I've been worried."

Garrett laughed. "Sit down. The doctor says I have a concussion and has gone to pull someone off the streets to keep me from going to sleep. Care to volunteer?"

"Really?" she asked, a smile brightening her face. "You're not mad at me?"

"I wouldn't go *that* far," he said, teasing her. "In my business, I'm well aware that accidents happen. I know you weren't out to harm anyone."

She shook her head, a tired smile on her full lips.

"Everyone is busy," Dr. Call said as he walked through the door. His scowl disappeared immediately when he saw Amber. "Oh, I didn't realize you had a…visitor. Good. That takes care of that. Should I keep calling your folks, or will your girlfriend be able to stay with you?"

Garrett didn't want to get Amber into more trouble. "Yes, please. Amber has had a long day."

The doctor gave her instructions on when to call the nurse and left the room. "You didn't have to..." She bit her lip, and leaned her head to one side, as if trying to avoid the attraction.

He reached out his hand, hoping she'd take it. "Maybe I'm the one who should be apologizing, for selfishly committing you to staying awhile longer to keep me from falling asleep."

"It's me that owes you. You kept me from getting into more trouble more than once tonight, and don't try to deny that." She took a hesitant step closer and took hold of his hand momentarily. "I can't tell you how much I regret the accident, Officer."

"If you're going to sneak in here under the pretense of my girlfriend and make sure I don't fall asleep, I think you'd better call me Garrett. Otherwise I'll have to call security, and neither of us needs to fill out any more reports tonight, do we?" He smiled, though he really wanted to go to sleep, despite the beautiful woman God had sent tonight to interrupt his life.

"I feel so foolish," she said quietly. She blinked away tears, and he could see these weren't her first of the evening. Her mascara was already smudged. "I should have done something to scare the guy away. Maybe the girl would be safe and sound in her dorm room now."

"No, you shouldn't have done any more. You definitely shouldn't. You could've been hurt. We don't know what the suspect's motive was. It might have been much worse. Don't blame yourself, Amber." He listened carefully for the next half hour as she talked through the incident, including the feeling that no one believed what she'd seen.

When the doctor came back into the emergency exam room a while later, he had Garrett's shift supervisor and his brother Nick with him.

Nick spoke first. "You okay?"

"Apparently not enough to get out of here."

The lieutenant looked at Amber and his smile faded. "How did you get in here?"

That look of fear returned instantly to Amber's face.

"It's okay, I approved her visit. In fact, I asked her to stay to keep me company until they could reach my folks to come take me home," Garrett confessed, hoping it wasn't going to cost him more than a little razzing from the guys. "It's my fault."

His brother studied Amber. "You own the bakery in Old Town, don't you? I think we met during the Harvest Festival, a few weeks ago."

"Yes, I own it, but it's not just a bakery, it's now Parties Galore, with party supplies and planning services, and costumes…" She studied his brother, then smiled as she apparently remembered meeting him. "Oh, yes," she said, looking at Garrett, then back to Nick. "You and a female officer made sure I got into the shop safely, didn't you? And then your partner came in and rented that chicken costume."

"That's right." He nodded, hiding a smile. "Things going okay?"

"Yes, it's been very quiet lately, since the festival

anyway. Thanks for watching out for all of us downtown." She looked sheepishly at him. "Garrett, since you have company, I'll say good-night," Amber said as she stood. "Stop in the shop sometime. Coffee and pastries are on me."

"Oh, wait," Garrett said. "Nick, Amber's a...party planner. He's the one who might need help...with a party."

Nick looked at Garrett as if he'd lost his mind.

"Sure...." She pulled a business card from her bag. "Give me a call. I guarantee I can give you a deal."

She made a quick exit, and Garrett hated to admit he didn't want to see her go.

The lieutenant glanced out of the ER room and waited a few minutes before speaking. "You let the woman who turtled you keep you company in the hospital?" he asked in disbelief.

"Someone had to do it. The doctor was looking for volunteers," Garrett replied, hoping Chavez was in a better mood than he looked. "I'm not kidding. She just happened to be in the wrong place at the wrong time twice tonight."

Nick glanced at their supervisor then back to Garrett. "Sounds like you'll heal, you're cranky enough to scare any real damage away," his brother said with a laugh, trying to lighten the mood.

"Did you find anything on the missing girl?"

Lieutenant Chavez shook his head. "I think Ms. Scott has an active imagination."

Nick's expression wasn't as clear. "There's still a BOLO out, so every officer in the county will be watching for her."

"May as well inform Wyoming by now. If I'd stuffed a body into a car, I wouldn't stick around," Garrett muttered.

"We took Ms. Scott to the location she recalls seeing the incident, but didn't find anything to support her claim of a struggle," his supervisor insisted.

"Not an abandoned car? Nothing?" His headache was getting worse. "It was in the area of the university, right? Maybe it was a coed who was going to work, or…"

"Ms. Scott insists the girl was getting into a yellow SUV. It was there, but the door was closed, and the vehicle is registered to a twenty-five-year-old male. We haven't located him yet," Lieutenant Chavez said. "We'll need to wait for a missing person report to come in."

Garrett looked at his brother in disbelief. Nick didn't look any happier than Garrett felt right now.

"Amber Scott saw something. She was not making it up." That woman couldn't lie if her life depended upon it. He'd stake his life on that. He just had to figure out how to convince the lieutenant to find the suspect before he hurt anyone else. Especially before he realized someone from Parties Galore actually had witnessed the crime.

FIVE

Amber waited in the hospital lobby for the victim's advocate from the police department to give her a ride home. At least then she'd have contact with the police if there was a problem at the shop.

The lieutenant hadn't looked too happy to see her there checking on Officer Matthews. If only he knew how she really felt about police officers, he'd realize she was genuinely concerned. She paced from one entrance to the other, watching for Samantha Taylor, anxious to have this night end.

She glanced at the clock on her cell phone. It had been half an hour since she'd called. Maybe dispatch hadn't gotten the message to her.

"Amber?" a deep voice said from behind her.

She recognized the voice and turned toward Garrett. "You're going home? That's a relief." He still looked very miserable.

"Yeah, Nick's going to drop me off at our folks' house so they can keep an eye on me. Dr. Call won't let me go home to an empty house. Could we give you a ride somewhere?"

Nick glanced at his watch, then to Amber. "Are you going to the bakery or home?"

She smiled. "Oh, the bakery is home now. My grandmother has moved to the senior center, so I'm the resident baker. After you and your partner scared the wits out of me that night, Bomma and I decided it was much safer for me to live there than come and go in the middle of the night." She shrugged. "I'm getting to like it. It saves a lot of time, and if I get a chance to take a few minutes to rest, I'm right there."

"Why don't we cancel your call for the VA and drop you off. We can make sure no one is hanging around," Nick said.

Amber saw a look of concern on Garrett's face. "I appreciate the offer, Nick, but I've already caused your brother enough trouble. The victim's advocate, Samantha, I think it was, said she'd give me a ride. You should get your brother home so he can rest."

Garrett's mouth formed an irresistibly devastating grin. "I appreciate your concern, but I'm going to be fine. It's no bother...."

Amber smiled back, wishing they'd met under better circumstances. The shadow of his beard accentuated the strength of his jaw. Even sitting in a wheelchair with his bulletproof vest across his lap he looked just as strong and virile as he had when he'd stood tall from his toppled vehicle. She pulled her mind back to their conversation and to the fact that he was a cop. "I hope you're right about being fine," she said, "but I don't think your boss was too pleased to see me here. I don't want to get you into any more trouble...." She knew she shouldn't let herself read anything into

Garrett's chivalry, but it wasn't easy. She hadn't had anyone look at her like that in months. Apparently she needed to dress up more often. Why, of all the men in the county, did the one to catch her attention have to be a cop?

From the corner of her eye Amber noticed the victim's advocate pull up to the door. "My ride's here. Take it easy, okay?" She hurried out the door and to the police car before she was tempted to accept their offer. She had a lot of problems to work through before the shop opened in the morning. Number one was getting Garrett Matthews off her mind.

She directed Samantha to the Old Town shops, uncomfortable with the thought of going into the dark building alone, tonight more than usual.

Samantha Taylor must have read her mind. "I'll go in with you, if that's okay, just to check things out."

"Sure," she said, "I'd appreciate it."

"So you're a party planner, huh?" the young woman asked. "Sounds interesting."

"That's a good way to describe it. No two parties come off the same," Amber said. "I mainly coordinate weddings, but I also help arrange engagement parties, anniversaries, and even a few extraordinary birthday bashes."

"Rumor has it Sergeant Matthews, the brother of the cop you ran into, is unofficially engaged to his trainee. I don't suppose they've contacted you to plan their wedding, have they?"

Amber had been caught off guard at the accident when Garrett had asked her if the wedding shower was for Sarah. She wasn't going to slip again. "I don't discuss my client list—sorry. I do have several people willing to give a reference if you're looking for a planner…."

"No, I was just curious. It's just surprising how Nick had been single all these years, and suddenly he falls for his trainee. At least there's still one eligible bachelor in the family, though from what I can tell, Garrett has his sights set on a bigger career than being a street cop. He doesn't bend any rules, especially when it comes to the job. And I never see him with the same woman twice. It's like he doesn't want any baggage holding him back. I'll just bet he's having a coronary over his brother's scandal!"

Amber wasn't sure how to respond. She wondered what in the world made Samantha tell her all that, or if her reaction to Garrett Matthews was that transparent. She felt ridiculous now for going to the hospital to check on him. He probably thought she was a stalker. At least Samantha had answered Amber's question of Garrett's interest.

It would go nowhere, and probably the best for both of them. She didn't have time for a relationship right now, either. She was so worn out, she just wanted to go home and away from everyone. "I suppose that's best if he realizes he's not willing to settle down and make a commitment. No need complicating things for anyone."

"I guess, though I'd love to change his mind about his priorities," Samantha said with a smile.

Amber let out a polite laugh, thankful that they were almost to the shop. "Turn left down the alley, to the third mercury light on the right. That's my door."

After Samantha checked the main level, she left. Amber didn't mention that her living quarters were actually upstairs. Surely if the cop didn't realize that, neither would an intruder. After all, it had a separate lock on it to assure the hired help wouldn't take liberties with her home.

Nothing was quite as reassuring as hearing the metal bolt on the steel door sliding into the latch. Her grandfather had installed a security alarm on the front of the shop several years back, when gangs started hanging out in the downtown area. Nana had managed to avoid making enemies with anyone, even the gang members, and Amber prayed she would be able to maintain a neutral relationship with them, as well.

Amber double-checked the alarm, then went upstairs to change into her baking clothes. Even though she was dead tired, she wasn't going to sleep well until she'd worked off some of this adrenaline. She at least needed to get the dough made and rising before she took a nap. Her phone rang after she'd changed. She checked the caller ID. It was Rachelle.

"Hi. How'd the shower go?"

"It was fun, sorry you had to miss it. I've been calling you for an hour now. What in the world took so long? Are you okay?"

"Yeah, just shook up," Amber said, then told her friend about the crime she'd witnessed. "I was following the car to try to get his license plate number when I ran into the cop. I couldn't believe it. The van just...scooped up the SUV and rolled it over, like it was made to do it. Then the SUV started spinning like a top."

Rachelle gasped. "Oh, my gosh, you toppled a cop? There were so many cars at the accident, I guess I thought there were more than the two vehicles involved. You're lucky you aren't in jail for assaulting an officer!"

Amber pressed her hand to her head to ward off the headache that was quickly coming on. "You can say that again. At least a dozen cops were there doing nothing more than glaring at me."

Her friend stifled a laugh. "Were they at least cute?"

Amber smiled, thinking of Garrett. Then she remembered him hanging upside down in the SUV, unable to get out, and the smile disappeared. "You're terrible. I nearly kill someone, and you're asking if the cops were cute. You know I'd never, ever, fall for a cop." Even as she made the vow, her stomach did flip-flops as she recalled how Garrett had flirted with her.

"I just asked if they were cute. There's no harm in looking, is there?"

"My mind wasn't on the cops…." *Not plural anyway,* she thought. "I had bigger concerns than them, believe it or not. Number one, that poor girl."

"Well, that goes without saying," she said, her voice turning serious. "Did the kidnapper see you? I mean your van's pretty hard to miss with balloons all over the side of it."

She tried to recall whether he'd looked in her direction. If he had seen her, what would he have done? Come after her? Had he rushed because he heard her? She felt sure it was unlikely he'd paid much attention to anything besides his victim. She wandered her apartment and looked out the windows.

"Amber? Are you sure you're okay?"

She let the curtain fall back into place. "Yeah. If he knew I was there, it wasn't obvious. He had all he could handle with the victim."

Rachelle let out a deep sigh. "I'm worried about you. Do you want to come over and stay here tonight?" She could hear clanging dishes in the background just before the baby started crying.

"Thanks, but I need to get my dough ready and figure out what I'm going to do about deliveries now."

"You can think here, where you'd be safe. I could send Tommy to come get you."

She wanted to laugh. "Oh, he'd love that at midnight. I'm safe here, Rachelle, but thanks. I'll see you in the morning, okay? I need to get busy, before I crash and burn." They said good-night after confirming arrangements for Rachelle to drop off her supplies the next morning.

Only problem was, Amber didn't crash and burn. She'd tried to go to sleep at three in the morning, but couldn't stop her mind from replaying the accident. She couldn't take her mind off that moment, and the officer who she'd hurt in her carelessness. She'd lain awake thinking of the tall, handsome officer who'd changed her mind about cops. She prayed over and over that Officer Matthews was okay. Prayed that the crime she'd witnessed was nothing more than a college prank. Prayed that the morning light would bring answers to her numerous concerns.

At six-thirty, the knock on the door nearly sent her through the roof. She'd already gone online and ordered wooden shutters for the glass-front windows to provide more security for the early-morning shift.

She looked out the peephole and opened the door for the two college girls who helped out around the shop. Thanks to the nervous energy, she'd finished the baking, leaving only glazing the pastries, brewing coffee, and filling display cabinets before the shop opened. While CiCi and Andrea washed up and put on their aprons, Amber filled them in on the challenges of the day, which were too numerous to ignore any longer. Time was getting away from her.

"Do you want me to deliver the day-old pastries to the shelter with my car?" CiCi offered. "I wouldn't want to put a full sheet cake in the hatchback, but we can box the pastries in the smaller boxes."

"That would be great. I have a couple of errands I need to run," Amber said as she scooped the coffee into the huge filter. "Sean should be here by seven-thirty to help with the before-work rush. I'll be gone most of the morning. Call if you have questions...."

The room was silent.

"Did I say something wrong?" she asked the two women. "Don't worry, I'm not asking to borrow your car. One of my stops is to rent a car for my own use. Rachelle is going to pick me up, and at the same time, deliver all of the supplies I picked up that were left in the van last night. I just hope the van is repaired before that huge wedding the weekend after next."

Andrea was folding the boxes and getting the bakery cases ready to fill with fresh pastries. "Unless the damage was pretty minor, I wouldn't bet on it. My dad's car took almost two months to fix after his accident."

Amber felt the weight of the world on her shoulders. This had been her grandparents' business. The memories here went deep—too deep to let go so easily. Especially not over a broken-down vehicle. Nana Scott had been ecstatic when Amber had asked if she could buy the bakery from her. Though her parents argued that she needed to go back to college and finish her degree, Amber was convinced that this was God's plan for her life. She was determined to prove to her parents that she could succeed without their help.

Amber yawned. "I have no idea how long it will take," she admitted, "but I don't know what we'll do if it's not repaired by then. I'll have to find some way to get the wedding cake to the resort. I cannot give up this order." The profit on it alone would pay this month's expenses, she mused. She'd had the van repainted and tuned up, hoping it would get her through a few more years while she got the new shop in the black financially. She just hoped they could make the repairs to keep it running. Another yawn escaped. This time Andrea and CiCi caught the wave of sleepiness.

"You haven't slept all night, have you?" Andrea asked.

Amber wondered if the half hour she dozed would really count as sleep. "I took a catnap, but it didn't help much. Since I finished decorating the cakes last night, I'll try to catch a little sleep after the lunch rush."

"Why don't you go sleep for a while now. We can get the rest of the cabinet shelves filled," CiCi said. "It looks like you have almost everything done for us. Once the coffee finishes brewing, we're about set. Then when Sean arrives to help Andrea, I'll make the deliveries."

There was a knock on the alley door.

"That's probably Rachelle," she said, taking a step toward the door. "The coffee is made, the cinnamon raisin loaves are cooling on the racks, but need to be sliced and bagged." She looked out the peephole and reached for the doorknob, then froze.

Amber opened the door, surprised to see Garrett's brother, Nick, still in uniform. Another officer was sitting in a separate car. "Morning, Ms. Scott. I'm Sergeant Nick Matthews…."

"Hi," she said tentatively, wondering why he was addressing her so formally after meeting at the hospital. "Is your brother okay?"

He looked at her oddly. "As far as I know, he's doing fine. Why?"

"Well, you're here, for one thing, and you sounded so official. Am I under arrest for something?"

He laughed. "No, sorry, the introduction is just a formality. We've been patrolling a little more by your shop through the night, and I noticed that you have some company. Since a white sedan showed up sometime in the last hour, I thought we'd better check on you."

Amber leaned just far enough out the door to see the white car. "It's here?"

"There's no one inside it, but we thought there was a chance that the guy may have noticed your van and placed you here…."

She glanced at Nick. "That's similar to the car I saw last night, but it's not as nice." She quickly stepped back inside her shop. "My employees just arrived. Do you want to see if it belongs to either of them?"

"That would probably be a good idea."

As Nick stepped inside, Amber worried that he was going to take her in to the station because of her old charges. Though her lawyer had assured her years ago that her record had been cleared, doubt still plagued her. "This is Andrea and CiCi."

As Sergeant Matthews questioned her employees, Amber studied him closer. Nick was taller and stockier than his brother, but it was Garrett's intriguing gray eyes that really caught her attention. He and Garrett had similar mannerisms, but that was where the resemblance ended. It was too bad she had such an aversion to police officers.

"Ms. Scott?"

She tore her mind from Garrett Matthews, and the temptation she had to ask Nick more questions about his brother. "Yes?"

"Lieutenant Chavez asked me to remind you to go by the precinct sometime today to look at mug shots and see if you can identify the suspect. If you do that, you'll need to talk to M.J. Daniels, our artist. She works from noon to five today. I figure we should get a description of the man you saw while it's fresh on your mind, just in case something does come of the case."

Realizing her nap was out of the question, she said, "Okay, so you never found the girl?"

He shook his head. "No sign of anyone fitting that description yet…. It's only been twelve hours, but if no one makes a report, our hands are tied."

Amber wrapped her arms around her body, feeling a chill of the cool autumn air at the reminder. "And the car in the alley?"

"Belongs to your employee, Andrea."

"Oh, I missed that, I guess...." *While I was dreaming about your brother.* "Thanks for checking in with us, Nick." Just then Rachelle pulled into the alley and approached very slowly. Nick got into the squad car and drove away.

She motioned her friend to pull up to the door, and waited to carry the boxes of costume accessories inside. "If it's slow this morning, you could price these and hang them up out front." Amber slipped the apron over her head, tossed it into the laundry hamper and ran up to change her clothes, then returned to finish telling her employees what needed to be done. "It seems like I'll be gone most of the day, so don't hesitate to call if you have questions." She wished she could stay home and hide in bed, but that was out of the question. Especially with a vehicle to replace.

"Where do you want me to put them? You're running out of space..." she heard CiCi say as she stepped out of the bakery, determined to get her life straightened out. She didn't have time to deal with insurance companies and police officers. Especially the one officer she couldn't seem to forget.

SIX

After Amber picked up the rental car, she drove to the Victorian Inn to pick up the plastic cake plates and see if anyone else knew anything about the girl who drove the yellow SUV.

She went from one business to the next, hoping someone would have seen something. "Do you know who drives the yellow SUV that's parked out there?"

"I've never seen it before. Who are you again?" People looked at her like she was crazy. The more she tried to explain, the crazier it sounded.

"I witnessed an incident outside here. I'm hoping someone else could help identify the victim. Do you have a tall, thin college-age woman who works here? She might have come in around five-thirty yesterday."

"No, we don't employ college students."

She had the same types of responses at every stop. Not one mentioned that the police had talked to them.

Unfortunately no one had seen or heard anything, and no one seemed interested or overly concerned.

She went from there to the police station and asked

for Officer Matthews. She needed to find out why no one had questioned local shop owners and their staff.

"He's off today." The uniformed officer behind the front desk looked like he was still in high school— fresh military haircut, clean-shaven face.

She didn't figure she'd have any luck, but asked anyway. "Do you know when he'll be back on duty?"

"I'm sorry, we can't give out that information."

Amber looked around, uneasy being here. "Can I speak with Officer Chavez? He was the officer who took my report last night."

"He's not on duty now, but if you'd like to leave your name and phone number, I'll give him your message."

Two days later Garrett waited impatiently to talk to the chief. His supervisor had called to check on him earlier in the day and had broken the news that he would be required to take a few more days off.

His soon-to-be sister-in-law, Sarah Roberts, walked by. "Sorry to hear about the accident, Garrett. How're you feeling?"

"I'm fine," he replied, careful about what he said. He wanted to stay on duty, but he knew from Nick and his narcotics officer brother, Kent, that the chief didn't like to be pushed with his back to a wall. "It's amazing what a difference a day makes. Yesterday I woke with a headache. Today it's gone. I feel great."

Sarah looked at him suspiciously. "It's only been two days, Garrett…."

The officer assigned to the front desk interrupted them, much to Garrett's relief. "Officer Matthews?"

"Yeah," Garrett responded, eager to stop Sarah from saying that the pain hadn't even reached its peak yet.

"There's a woman here to see you."

"Me?" Garrett glanced at the chief's secretary, then to Sarah. "Did she say what she needs?"

"Just said she needs to see you. She's come in here the past two days asking to speak to you. I don't know that she'll take no for an answer again."

"I'll be down in a few minutes," Garrett said, hoping the chief would be available quickly. "Sarah, I'll see you at Mom and Dad's tomorrow for Sunday dinner. It'll be the first time in a long time we've all been off at the same meal."

"That's not to be taken for granted, then, is it? I'll see you later, Garrett. Take it easy," Sarah said.

He looked at the secretary, and she seemed to know his silent plea.

"He's still on the phone, Officer Matthews. I'll let him know that you're waiting to see him if you want to take care of your other business."

He glanced at the red light on her phone and nodded. He may as well find out who was so desperate to talk to him. Though he was positive it was Amber. "I'll be right back."

"I'm sure you will be," the secretary said with a smile.

He stepped through the door to the lobby, and immediately recognized the woman who had thrown a major kink in his plans. "Hello, Ms. Scott."

Worry lines dissipated from her face and he realized she was every bit as pretty as he'd remembered. She jumped to her feet. "Hi. You're okay," she said softly.

"I was getting worried when they said you were off duty for a while. I hope it's nothing serious."

"Who told you that?"

"Your brother. He and his girlfriend stopped by the shop this morning to talk about a wedding cake and to make sure I'm doing okay."

Figures, Garrett thought. "And are you?"

"I'm just fine. That's what I needed to find out about you."

"Good," he said awkwardly. "I'm hoping to come back to work soon. I'm more than ready."

She smiled, her full lips quirked to one side. "That's such a relief. I know you're probably busy, but I wanted to see if they ever found the car, or if the girl… I can't get any information from anyone else. Nick said it sometimes takes days for people to report someone missing. I'm just sure…"

He shook his head, wishing it was easier to ignore the sincere concern in her brilliant blue eyes. "I haven't heard anything about the case since I'm on mandatory leave." *Thanks to you.* He tried not to think it. Tried not to blame her.

He tried not to think of her, period. He had to get his career back on track as soon as possible. He had to get back in the game if he stood a chance of getting hired with the Drug Enforcement Administration or the Federal Bureau of Investigation. He'd made it past the first cut for both.

"I keep trying not to think about it, but once I get something in my head, I can't get it out until I've done everything I can to solve it."

"It's not your problem, though."

"It is when I'm the witness. And from the responses I received from the people who work near the Vioto llan Inn, I'm the only one who saw anything. My parents think I'm a little too driven. Giving up isn't easy for me. And I keep seeing that poor woman...." She looked at him with her big blue eyes. His heart skipped a beat.

He didn't want to acknowledge the paradoxical feelings toward this woman and the guilt she was likely experiencing. She felt responsible. She wanted to help.

How could he resent her and her following up on her concerns? She'd been following her convictions to help. Her convictions were no different than his reasons for going into law enforcement. Her intentions to help a victim of a crime were from the heart. He had to respect that, if nothing else.

"If it were my sister, I wouldn't want anyone to walk away without trying to help her..." she said, her voice softening. "Someone is missing her, I just know they are. Why aren't the police looking for her?"

That was all he needed to melt his resolve. He and his family had felt the same way when his sister had needed protection. Just like Kira, Amber wasn't going to give up. And she was right. They couldn't ignore a credible witness. "How do you know they aren't?"

"How do you know they *are?*"

He didn't, but her assumption that they weren't doing anything stopped him cold. This wasn't the place to argue with a witness. He wanted nothing more than to defend the department, but he had nothing to go on.

"I'm waiting to talk to the Chief of Police. I'll see what I can find out." He felt his pockets for something to write with, then looked around for a piece of paper, finding none. He hadn't come prepared to work. His notebook was in his locker, two floors down. He glanced at her, wondering if she had any clue how difficult it was to concentrate with her around. "I presume your contact information is in the accident report."

She got a look of panic on her face. "Ummm, I'm sure it is, I mean, I gave it to the officer that night." Amber Scott reached into the massive purse hanging from her shoulder. "Here, I'll make it easy for you," she said, handing him a business card with balloons and wedding bells on it.

"Parties Galore? I'm not familiar with it."

"It's the new name for my grandmother's bakery, It was Candy and Confections…in Old Town…."

"Oh, sure. Mom used to get cakes from there all the time…" Realizing he'd practically insulted her grandmother's business. "For our birthday parties," he said, digging a deeper hole for himself to get out of. She waited silently, not about to give him an easy out. "Birthday parties are pretty low-key these days…."

"I could fix that, if you'd like," she said with a smirk. "I am a party planner."

Garrett felt his skin warm up, and hoped it wasn't obvious how embarrassed he was. He held up the card. "A party planner, when you're not a private investigator, huh?"

Amber shot him a coy smile. "I'll have to see how this case pans out. A side business might be fun." She smiled, completely knocking him off balance.

The officer at the front window interrupted, his voice squawking through the speaker in the bullet-proof glass. "Garrett, the chief is available now...."

"Call me," she said simply and turned to leave.

"Yeah, I will. You be careful," he said awkwardly, making a beeline up the stairs, trying to run from the unwelcome feelings he was fighting.

His plans for the future left no room for complications. Women fit into the complication category. Amber Scott fit into the women category.

He was in trouble.

Amber Scott had already thrown a monkey wrench into his chances of joining the FBI or DEA. He didn't need to make matters worse by getting emotionally involved with her, too.

He needed to find answers to her suspicions right away so he could focus on his goals. Until then, he wasn't going to be able to concentrate on anything but her. Her safety. That was all he needed to concern himself with.

He'd find some logical explanation for what she saw that night. She'd be happy. He'd get on with his life and he'd be happy, too. He made a beeline for the chief's office.

"Garrett," Chief Thomas said a minute later, offering his hand.

Garrett knew it was going to hurt like crazy to shake the chief's hand, but a man had to do what it took to get back to work. *No pain, no gain.* He wasn't about to sit out of the action because of a stiff neck.

He grasped the chief's hand firmly, steeling himself. Chief Thomas shook his hand vigorously, then glanced at him suspiciously. "I wish I had more officers determined to get back to work like you are, Garrett." He motioned him into his office and let the door close behind them. "You're not going to do me much good out on the streets with less than one hundred percent mobility."

He'd failed again. "It's not that bad," Garrett said lamely. Seeing the look of contempt in the chief's eyes, he dropped Plan A and moved on to Plan B. "I could help in the office or on the investigation, then."

"What investigation? Your accident…?"

"The police impersonator, the missing girl—this isn't the first…" Garrett said, as if it were the only investigation they had in the department. "What do we have on it so far?"

"Not much. You focus on that shoulder, Matthews."

"My shoulders and neck and everything else are fine, sir."

The chief shook his head. "Even *my* hands are tied on this one, Garrett. No one has been reported missing. The car hasn't turned up…."

Garrett suspected as much. The case was essentially closed. "I believe Ms. Scott, Chief. She hasn't changed the details, her story makes sense. This isn't the first report we've had of suspicions police impersonators. They *have* to be tied to each other. Has any warning been issued to the public?"

"The mayor won't allow it. He feels we've just gained some of the community's confidence again after the rapist was caught. Asking an open-ended question about a missing girl is opening Pandora's box. And he doesn't want to cast any more shadows over the police department by bringing up a police impersonator. It's not going to happen."

Garrett thought about Plan C. He hadn't thought he'd need Plan C. "So we're just dropping the case?"

The chief pulled a folder from the stack on his desk and opened it up, silently studying it. "I know you're looking to move into a new career, Garrett, and I think you have an outstanding chance of being hired with any one of the federal agencies."

Garrett felt a "but" coming. "Yes, sir, I have. Thank you for your vote of confidence, but at this point, that's nothing more than a pipedream. I have time on my hands, and I need to find this creep."

"I'm not going to let you back out on the streets before your neck has a chance to heal. You need to be one hundred percent ready when the DEA or FBI call you to test."

Garrett's mind wandered. He hadn't thought of how he'd test with a sore neck and shoulder. It was hurting more than yesterday and far more than he'd hoped it would be by today. He had been applying ice bags and heat alternately so he'd have no medications in his system. Maybe he'd look into some other treatments to speed things along.

"I know you want to be working on this case, Garrett, but…it wouldn't be in your best interest to pursue this investigation."

Garrett couldn't believe what Chief Thomas had just said. Since when did they only investigate the cases that were interesting, or convenient? "Okay, if someone else is looking into it, let me do something to help. I could go through old files, whatever. Maybe one of our old applicants is holding a grudge. Even office work and phone calls would keep me from going stir crazy at home. Anything."

Chief Thomas stared at Garrett as if he'd said something wrong. He stood and looked out the window, muttering something like "Another hotshot Matthews."

"Excuse me, sir. Did you say something?"

He shook his head. Finally he looked Garrett in the eye and spoke. "I do have something you can do. Ms. Scott has been very persistent about this missing girl. She arrived at the scene the next morning, started asking questions of every shop owner in the area. I want you to keep her quiet and out of our hair until she loses interest in the case."

Garrett couldn't believe what he was hearing. "What? I thought you said…"

"I don't doubt she saw something, but it has been just over forty-eight hours. I'm beginning to think that it was a boyfriend and girlfriend arguing or a college prank. We don't have enough to go on right now. Business in the university area is just starting to recover."

While the chief said something about the newspapers, Garrett's mind was spinning, desperate to come up with a Plan C. Anything to keep from facing those big blue eyes with a scheme to keep her quiet. He should say something to keep the chief from reading the wrong thing into his silence.

"Amber Scott seems very defensive every time one of our uniformed officers talks to her, but I understand that night after the incident, she came to visit you at the hospital. Apparently she seems pretty comfortable talking to you."

Garrett's brain had stopped registering after the chief ordered him to keep Amber out of their hair for a few days.

"How well do you know her, Matthews?" the chief asked.

The last thing he needed right now was to get to know her better. "I don't," he said—not that he didn't *want* to know Amber Scott. What he needed was to get back on duty where he could find out what was happening with the investigation. He needed to figure out why they were throwing this case out with the trash.

The chief's commanding voice broke into his thoughts. "Care to explain why she showed up at the hospital, if you've never met her before?"

He came up with a response that the chief would want to hear. "She came to visit because she felt guilty, sir."

The chief nodded, erasing a smile as soon as it flashed on his mouth. "Good—that makes your job easier. What about her visit just now? Did she ask about the missing girl?" The chief was not happy with Amber Scott.

Nothing was a secret around here. "Yes, apparently no one here would tell her anything about the case. So yes, she's not only concerned about me, but the female victim. As we all should be, shouldn't we?"

The captain shot him a silent reprimand that instantly let Garrett know he'd pushed too far. Chief Thomas picked up a file and opened it. The quieter he got, the harder Garrett's brain worked to figure out how he could survive this assignment. He hadn't seen this coming.

"We have investigators looking at the reports of

police impersonators, Garrett. They will make any necessary inquiries. Your assignment right now is to keep Amber Scott quiet. She likes you and you're our best chance to keep her out of the way so we can sort through this."

Nick had been set up by two fellow officers. Was Garrett next? But how could anyone have set this up? There's no way someone could have planned for Amber to run him off the road. Besides, what could they be setting him up for? It didn't make any sense. Not that the bad guys ever made sense.

How was he supposed to ignore Amber Scott? She was gorgeous, had a strong conscience and she now had information that could frighten the wrong people. No matter what his own plans were, he couldn't stand to let her face this alone. The chief was right about one thing: there had been some sort of connection between him and Amber that night.

There wasn't an officer at the accident who hadn't given him grief about letting a good-looking woman turn him upside down. Now the chief was sending him back for more razzing?

He leaned back in his chair, studying the Chief of Police. "You're serious, aren't you?" he asked the chief, just to be sure it wasn't some initiation prank.

The chief zeroed in on Garrett and nodded. "I am. You're not going out on the streets yet, Matthews. So far, we have no indication that Amber Scott is in danger, but if she draws more attention to herself and this incident, she may have more than *our* interest, real quick. And I don't want another victim."

Garrett couldn't believe they weren't paying more

attention to this case. "And what if this creep goes after our only witness? How can we have nothing to go into an investigation on? How can that be?"

The chief ignored his question. "This will go on your record as witness protection service. Be sure to add that to your résumé."

He was ready to argue—until the chief turned it to benefit his career aspirations. "What are we protecting her from, exactly, since she witnessed a crime that we're not investigating?"

"I didn't say nothing happened. And I definitely didn't say no one is investigating. I said Lieutenant Chavez found no evidence to investigate...." He paused, as if he wanted to say more, but letting Garrett know he'd been out of line.

Garrett worked to hold his temper. He played this through his mind again. What was the chief really saying? Did he suspect a cover-up? If so, why wasn't he calling in someone with more experience than he had to look into it?

The chief tapped his finger on another file and rubbed his forehead while Garrett waited for him to say something. He seemed deep in thought as he opened the file and read the rap sheet.

Garrett tried, but couldn't make out a name on the file or the paperwork. "Is there something more I need to be aware of?"

He read a little further and closed the manila folder. "Not at this time," he said with that abruptness that Garrett had learned from his father not to question. It was never a good sign when the chief himself gave you an order. "I'm not asking you to do anything more than keep Ms. Scott out of harm's way, Garrett. But if anything at all comes to your attention, I expect you to come to me and only me."

Garrett felt the pain deepen. Though he didn't dare say it, this had scandal written all over it. "And how do you suggest I explain myself hanging around her shop? I'm not thrilled with telling her that I'm trying to keep her out of the police's way when we're not pursuing an investigation."

The chief tapped the police file, not looking a bit sympathetic. "The one thing I wouldn't tell Ms. Scott is that you're there to keep her out of our way. You want to hit the big leagues, now's your chance to see if you have what it takes to go undercover. Say whatever you feel right telling her, Matthews. Just keep her out of our way, and don't let her talk to the press. I don't need the city in another state of panic."

SEVEN

Amber hadn't had energy to waste worrying about why Officer Matthews hadn't called after his talk with the chief. It had been a busy afternoon, even for a Saturday and she'd had too much to do to get ready for Maya Brewer's wedding to waste time thinking about a cop. By the time the shop closed, she was dead tired and wanted nothing more than to sleep. She had a couple of errands to run before she could call it a night. It had been a long week and she hadn't had any rest since the accident.

On her way home she stopped at the grocery store for some perishables. By the time she pulled into the alley, the night had turned cold and damp, and a light snow was falling. As she drove into the alley, she wasn't pleased to find a group of kids lingering close enough to cause her concern. "Dear Lord, please protect me and place Your shield around the shop as I work to honor You and my family through my business." She drove on past and around a few blocks, giving them time to move on. When she returned the alley was empty. She pulled into the parking nook and hurried to carry the bags inside.

She glanced at the blinking light on the business

line and wondered if Garrett had called. She listened to the messages, most of which had been hang-ups, then put the groceries away and went up to bed. She wanted to be refreshed and awake for church services, and since Sunday was her only real day off, she wasn't about to spend it sleeping.

Amber turned on the television, and sat down with a serving of French bread pizza.

She woke a few hours later to the sound of the shop's security alarm. As she jumped up, her plate crashed to the floor, shattering when it hit the coffee table on the way. She stumbled past the glass and ran to her front door. As she heard sirens in the distance, she realized she didn't dare go downstairs. What if whoever had broken in was still there? Hurrying toward the door, she wondered what had happened. Had the kidnapper finally figured out she'd seen him?

Seconds later her phone rang. She double-checked the lock on her apartment and ran to the kitchen, where her wall-mounted phone was. She tentatively answered, wishing again that she had caller ID.

"This is Rocky Mountain Security. We received an alarm from your shop. Are you okay?"

"Yes, I'm upstairs in my apartment. Do you know what happened?"

"Not exactly, but we've already sent the police. According to your file, this is in a business area and they're first on your call list, right?"

"Yes, that's right." That had been Nana's arrangement.

"Is there anyone there with you?"

"No. I don't really want to go down...."

"No, you make sure the doors are locked and stay on the line with us. The police should be there any time."

She made her way to the window above the front of the shop and peeked out, hoping to see the police. Dozens of people were gathered across the street, watching and pointing in her direction. She opened the window and sniffed, hoping there wasn't a fire burning below her.

"Ms. Scott?" the security operator asked.

"Yes," she said, remembering the phone tethering her to the kitchen. "I'm here."

"Do you hear any noises from the shop?"

"No, but I looked out the window and there are a lot of people watching and pointing. Something obviously happened."

Surely the burglar had run by now. She had turned to open the door when she saw the flashing lights of the police car approaching. She looked through the peephole, then quickly turned on the stairs light.

"I see the police have arrived, but I don't have a cordless phone on this line. Should I…?"

"Can you communicate with the police through a window before opening your door?"

She moved back to the window. "Yes, just a minute."

Amber lifted the window lock and cranked the window open. "Officer, I'm the owner of the party store. The security company is on the line…."

The officer looked up and help up a hand to quiet her. "Just a minute," he said, then came back to her. "Sorry about that—another officer was reporting from the back of the shop. It's quiet back there. It appears someone broke the front window, but we can't get in, so I presume you're safe to come down."

"Oh," she said, realizing she was still barefoot. "Just a minute, and I'll be down." She reported to the security company, and by remote they turned off the annoying alarm.

She went back to the couch and shook her head at the mess, then slipped on her clogs and hurried downstairs to let the police in.

Since she came to the back door first, she looked out, then tentatively opened the door, wondering who was on call tonight. She hadn't met this officer before. He introduced himself. "I'm Officer Jared Daniels. Are you the owner?"

She nodded. "I'm Amber Scott…"

"Oh, yeah, I recognize the name," he said, taking a second look. "Are you okay?" he asked.

Amber nodded.

He lifted his hand to his chest and pressed the button of a tiny mike in his buttonhole. After repeating her name three times in response to different questions, he turned his attention back to her. "Let's see what the damage is."

Her uneasiness tripled with the news that even officers she hadn't met knew her name. Was she on every cop's target list now? She stepped farther away from Officer Daniels. "The broken window is most likely in the lobby," she said, pointing toward the front of the store.

"Wait here a minute, Ms. Scott. Let me check it out." He pulled his weapon and eased his way to the front. "Looks okay. Come on in."

She followed him, which was much less threatening. Peering around him, she saw the hole in the window, and a baseball-size rock on the lobby floor. A bitterly cold wind blew inside.

A third police car arrived and stopped in the middle of the street.

"Don't touch anything," Officer Daniels reminded her as he reached for the door. "Do you have any plywood around that we could use to close this up?"

"That's locked—let me get the key." She hurried back to the kitchen, then opened the door for the other officers. She didn't recognize any of them, but they all looked at her as if they knew her. By name, anyway.

"Any wood?" Officer Daniels repeated.

"My grandfather may have left something in the cellar. He was always fixing things for Nana."

"Are they here now?"

"My grandfather? No, I've taken over the bakery. Papa died several years ago. In fact, he's the one who put the security system in."

Outside, a blue Mustang screeched to a stop next to the police car and Garrett Matthews rushed inside. "Are you okay?"

"Yes, I was upstairs."

He gave her an odd look, and the on-duty officers stepped back, as if to give him space. "How long have you been home?"

"A while, I guess. Why?" Amber asked, glancing from Garrett to the other officer.

Garrett stuffed his hands into his jeans pockets and stared at her. "I came by a while ago to fill you in on…"

"Oh, I'm sorry I missed you." She glanced at the officer and smiled. "I guess you already knew—I'm the one who ran into Officer Matthews."

Officer Daniels smiled back. "Garrett's my cousin, so yeah, I know all about it. Still, we'll need to figure out if this case was random, or if it might be related. So can you tell me more about what happened?"

Garrett had started pacing the room. "Yeah, where were you? Why didn't you answer the door?"

"I woke up to the sound of the alarm, so I'm not sure how long I was asleep or what time it is, even. I closed the shop at five and ran a few errands, so I was gone for an hour or two maybe."

"What—" Garrett's cousin started to ask another question when Garrett interrupted.

"It was longer than that. Did you go out and come home alone, or was someone with you?" Garrett crossed his arms over his chest.

The officer looked at Garrett and laughed. "Well, that's subtle."

Garrett shrugged his shoulders. "What? I needed to talk to her about the case."

Amber felt her heart flutter for a moment as she realized he was really concerned about her. Question was, was his interest personal as well as professional? "I was, and still am here alone—besides you, I mean. There were some guys standing outside the pub, so I drove on by and came back a few minutes later."

Garrett stopped pacing and bent to look at the rock, studying it from all directions without touching it. "Have you seen them around here before?"

"It's rather hard to tell whether it's the neighborhood kids or not with their hoods over their faces." She glared at him. "I try not to confront them, hoping they'll leave me alone. Nana always managed fine."

"Your grandmother wasn't—" Garrett started to say something, but his cousin interrupted this time.

"She was very fortunate," Officer Daniels said, pushing his cousin aside. "Garrett, let us investigate. Why don't you two go see if there's something to cover this hole for the night?"

Garrett glanced up before standing. "It looks like there's something written on this."

"We'll handle it, Gar," Jared said, nodding for them to get lost.

"So show me where this wood might be."

Amber led the way to the cellar, comforted to have him with her. "How'd you know this happened?"

"The shift commander called me. He seems to believe it's related to the kidnapping you witnessed. Apparently the chief told the commander about my meeting with him today. You shouldn't stay here, Amber. Not alone, anyway."

She pulled the string to turn on the light and showed him where her grandfather's workshop was. "Here's everything." She pulled a couple of wooden carts out of the way. "I don't see…"

"Amber…"

She didn't want to admit that she'd already started thinking of someone she could call. "What time is it?" She'd never get any sleep after this, but Rachelle had gone out of town to visit her parents for the weekend, and worrying Nana with this was out of the question.

Garrett looked at his watch. "Eleven-fifteen. Do you have someone you can stay with tonight?"

"It's kind of late to be calling people," she said hesitantly. "I'll be fine upstairs."

"The chief won't go for that," Garrett said simply. "We need to find a safe place for you to stay, and it would be best if it's not a friend's home where whoever did this could have seen you go before. You don't want to endanger them."

Amber simply stared at him. "Well, then, that doesn't leave me many options, does it? I wouldn't want to cause anyone else any trouble. Where does that leave me? Jail?"

"I wasn't thinking of that," Garrett said, with a smile teasing his lips. "I was thinking of my parents' house. They have several extra rooms. You'd be safe there. And they're used to unexpected emergencies."

"No offense, but I don't even know you, let alone your parents. Thank you, but I'll be fine. Let's find something to close up the window for a few days."

"My sister, then? I'd offer my brother's place, but…"

She spun around, disarmed to see the smile on his face. He had his arms folded across his chest and was leaning against the washing machine, just waiting for her to lose her temper. "You're kidding me?"

He chuckled. "No, I'm not kidding you, Amber. But I am trying to figure out what the chief's going to say when I show up to put you into a jail cell because you're refusing protective custody."

"I need to go to church tomorrow. I can't be in protective custody. I have a wedding to plan for next weekend," she said, rambling off a list of boring things in her hectic life.

He stepped close, and the smile disappeared. "You really don't have any other options, Amber. I'm not going to stay here with you alone, there's a hole in your window and snow's coming in. It's freezing up there."

"But…"

"You've already as much as admitted you don't *have* to be here at three in the morning to bake, so you may as well be somewhere you can get some rest, knowing that someone else is watching out for your safety. My parents' house has plenty of room—it's no inconvenience to them. You'll have privacy and protection. They go to church every week, so their schedule shouldn't impact your plans, as long as you understand I'm going with you to church."

"But…" she said, trying to come up with another plan. "I have lunch with my grandmother tomorrow."

"I'll be a perfect gentleman, Amber. I like grandmothers. And generally, most of them like me, too."

That's what I'm afraid of. "I don't want Nana to know anything about this, though. And if you come along, she'll be suspicious."

"She doesn't have to know I'm a cop. I could be a boyfriend."

"No!" She hadn't meant to say it so loud. "I mean, then she'd…no. You just cannot go to lunch with us."

Garrett laughed. "You're afraid she'll like me, aren't you?"

Amber struggled to keep the smile under wraps. "You know how grandmothers can be. She gets these wild ideas and there's no stopping her…." She felt her heart race. He didn't look sympathetic at all.

"You don't think she's going to read it in the newspaper? Amber, she lived here until, when? Last month? She knows what you're living with."

"Yes, she knows it's a concern, but no, she didn't hear anyone when she was upstairs. She's not deaf, but she doesn't hear well. She'll blame herself for selling to me. Can't you ask the police to keep it out of the news? It wasn't a break-in—not really, I mean. No one got in."

He moved to the stacks of wood and thumbed through them. "We don't know what it was yet, but I'll try to convince them to keep the details quiet, for your safety, if you'll cooperate…."

She let out a sigh of exasperation, and Garrett turned toward her.

"Amber, you can't keep burning the midnight oil worrying about whether you're going to wake up to someone in your shop waiting for you."

She wrapped her hands over her arms, hugging herself. She looked terrible after three nights without sleep, and she knew it. He was being nice. "If I agree to go to your parents', will you drop the church service and lunch with Nana? Please."

"How about if I'm an old friend who just dropped in? From college."

"Garrett, she did your birthday cakes. She may be losing her hearing, but she's not lost her memory. Garrett isn't that common a name, and her memory for customers is impeccable. Same for church. You're bound to know someone, and it's just awkward—a guy and a girl going to church together when they're not a couple. Everyone jumps to conclusions. And I really need to go to church today. I need to…"

"I understand, more than you think. You want somewhere you feel safe and protected. Where nothing bad can happen."

"Exactly," she said, relieved that he did understand. "I need to feel at peace."

"Bad things can happen in churches, too, Amber. And whether I'm with you, or just following you like a stalker, I will be there to make sure the kidnapper isn't." He turned, found some corrugated cardboard and sliced a large panel off. "Now, let's get the window covered and get you packed."

Later, as they drove across town to his parents' house in awkward silence, Amber came to one conclusion.

She had her life and issues. If she spent any more time asking questions about the crime she'd witnessed, she wouldn't have time to do her own work. *Help me leave that to You, Lord. Protect the girl,* she thought as a shiver spread through her body. *Bring the kidnapper to justice.*

EIGHT

Whatever apprehension Amber had at meeting and staying with Garrett's parents dissipated the minute they greeted her at the door. "Hi, Amber," his mother said. "We hope you can get some rest here."

"Thank you for letting me intrude. I hope it won't be any trouble." She glanced at his father, then back to his mom.

"Come in out of the snow," his dad prompted. "I'm Ted. Nice to see Garrett had the wisdom to get you out of harm's way. That downtown area has been sliding into dangerous territory for some years now. It's definitely not a safe place for a single young woman to be living alone."

Ted and Grace Matthews were an attractive couple, and she could see a lot of his father's features in Garrett. He would always be blessed with his good looks, apparently.

"So Garrett tells me. But despite that, as soon as I have the repairs made and the security system on again, I'll be out of your way. In the meantime…"

"There's no rush, Amber. Your grandmother went out of her way for me many times. Especially with changing the date for Kira's wedding not once, but twice. I'm glad to repay the favor. And I'm so relieved that you're keeping her shop open."

Garrett lifted Amber's bag and asked which room they wanted Amber to stay in.

"I've put all the wedding things away now, so Kira's room is fine. I think it's the most comfortable room for her, don't you?"

Garrett nodded. "That's fine. I'll be staying in my old room, if you don't mind. And since we all have church in a few hours, we'd better show her to her room."

His dad locked the front door, waiting for the rest of them to get upstairs before turning out the lights.

"It's late, so I'll give you the full tour in the morning," he said softly, giving her a wink as he disappeared into his bedroom.

"We'll have a light breakfast around eight, if you'd like to join us," his mother said. "But if you have the chance to sleep in, go right ahead. We'll try not to wake you. Will you be around for lunch?"

"No, thank you. I have plans to eat with my grandmother."

"If you'd like to eat here, I've made plenty. And your grandmother is welcome to join us, as well. Don't answer now—just think about it."

She took a quick shower, put on her pajamas and crawled into bed. It had been such a long week, and she couldn't believe she was finally at peace in the family home of the man she'd run into. She knew the chances that he'd kept her identity as the driver were slim to none. If he and his brother were both cops, it was unlikely that they'd keep that kind of thing a secret. Yet still, they'd welcomed her. And felt loved and safe and everything Garrett had promised. Would his family ever cease to surprise her?

She fell asleep within minutes, and slept clear through church. When she woke at eleven in the morning, she quickly dressed and hurried into the hallway. Garrett's door was open.

Peace and quiet surrounded her. She headed for the stairs and he greeted her at the base, holding a tiny white fluffy dog.

"I'm sorry I overslept. I haven't slept this late in years." The dog took one look at her and jumped out of Garrett's arms, landing on the nearest stair.

"That's PomPom." He smiled.

She sat on the steps and let the dog sniff her. He jumped into her lap to greet her, licking her face.

"PomPom, no! Sorry about that," he exclaimed, pulling the dog into his arms.

"I'll survive. She's much friendlier than most little dogs," she said, standing.

His eyes greeted her just as warmly. "I guess you pass the PomPom test. She's a good judge of character."

Amber wasn't sure how to respond to his comment that she'd passed any kind of test, let alone one given by the family pet. There was so much they didn't know about each other, and she couldn't help but wonder if they'd ever get the chance to move beyond this awkward stage. "I hope you realize what an incredible family you have, Garrett. I thought I'd be kicked out because of running into you. Instead, they opened their home to me. I don't remember resting this peacefully in weeks." She couldn't believe she'd confessed that. Her insomnia had started when she'd moved in with her grandmother. That couldn't be a coincidence.

"You needed it. I'm glad you came here, aren't you?"

He looked more rested, too, and she was thankful that she'd given in, if only to let him get some rest. She'd forgotten that he'd been putting in extra hours, as well. "I am. Thank you for insisting."

"I'll have to insist more often, if it's that easy." He smiled, that slow, lazy smile that set the butterflies in her stomach free. "I made some biscuits, eggs and bacon, if you'd like some. I tried to keep them warm in the oven, but I'm not sure they're still edible."

Amber needed to eat. "*You* made them? Or your mother did?" she asked, unable to believe cooking was also among this man's irresistible attributes.

"The eggs and bacon I can handle, but I confess, the biscuits are fresh from the oven, by way of the freezer."

Amber followed him into the kitchen, envious that he had a family straight out of a fairy tale. While she was eating, he set out an array of drinks to choose from, including a basket of tea or cocoa.

"Mom and Dad will be home from church soon. About lunch, I explained to my parents about you not wanting your grandmother to know about the problems at the store. I think it would be easier to keep it quiet with fewer people to spill the beans, but I'll go with your decision, as long as I'm included."

"You're probably right. Nana will be suspicious if I show up with you, but if we bring her here, there'd be no hope of convincing her that there's nothing happening."

He nodded silently.

"I need to go by the shop and do some cleaning and work before I go in to bake tonight. I can't tell you how much I appreciate this, Garrett." She heard the door close and his parents joined them, shaking snow off their coats and boots.

"Good afternoon, sleepyheads," his dad teased, a bright smile on his face. "You both look a little better after getting some rest."

Garrett took the pressure off her. "It's amazing how that works, isn't it? I know it's late notice, Mom, but we won't be here for lunch. I want to keep an eye on Amber, and she wants to check on the shop before we take her grandmother to lunch."

"You might want to take the SUV or van. Your car has a flat tire."

"Another one?" Garrett said. "I just got the last tire repaired two days ago."

"When did the last one happen?" his dad asked.

Garrett paused. "A couple of days before the accident. I took the car in to get new tires Friday. It's a brand-new tire."

Ted Matthews reached into his pocket and tossed Garrett the keys. "I'll look into it. You two get going."

"Thanks. We should be home later this evening."

His mother nodded. "Be careful, Garrett. And Amber, tell your grandmother hello for me."

Amber felt relief wash through her as she lifted the glass of grape juice to her lips to wash down the biscuit. She finished her bite and carried her empty plate to the sink. "Thank you again, Mr. and Mrs. Matthews. Garrett, let me go get my bag."

"Don't start this over, Amber. I insist you stay here until we have more answers."

She forced a smile. "And I insist I'll be fine at home. I'm not fond of facing that alley at two in the morning."

"Soon enough, you'll be back at the store, Amber. But not without a working security system. A few more nights of some real sleep will be good for you. And I'm going to be going in with you, so you won't have to face the alley alone. It's going to be okay. Call your grandmother and let's get going."

They introduced Garrett as simply a friend, and Nana was surprisingly low-key about it. Amber and Garrett were headed back to his parents' house after cleaning up the broken glass and adding another layer of tape and cardboard to the window when Nana called. Being a gentleman, he'd turned off the car radio when her phone rang. Nana called her to clarify that she'd heard all about her accident and the gang problems from one of the other seniors. When she started complaining about the gang problems, Amber turned the volume of her cell down, hoping to keep the conversation from Garrett. "I know Garrett and his brothers are police officers, Amber. But they're good men that you can trust, honey," she said over and over. "Don't let Garrett leave you there alone until they've found that kidnapper and the thug who broke our window," Nana emphasized.

"I don't really have much choice about that, Nana. We just left the shop and are on the way to Mr. and Mrs. Matthews' house now."

"If you have trouble with the insurance company, you let me know. Your grandfather put that security in to make them happy," she said, saying all the things that Amber had expected at lunch.

She was finally able to end the phone call.

Garrett was silent for a minute before teasing her. "I told you grandmothers like me."

"So we were both right," she said simply. "I knew she'd like you, and that she'd read more into this than there is."

Silence again filled the vehicle as he navigated the icy roads. She began to wonder if they would have hit it off as well if they had met under better circumstances.

"Without making it too obvious, can you see if you recognize the car two vehicles back? It's been behind us since we left the store."

She twisted to look and mostly saw snow-covered vehicles. "It looks like the same model as the kidnapper from what I can tell, but if he doesn't have a garage, how did he disappear so quickly that night?"

"Good question," he said, peering into the mirror. "Hang on, I'm going to turn the corner and flip a U-turn so we can try to identify him."

Amber's heart raced as she braced herself against the dash and the door. He turned the corner and started the turn, but a car was coming and he had to abandon the plan.

Before they could turn around to get behind the car, it was long gone.

When Andrea and Sean arrived Monday morning, Garrett was there, posing as their new coworker. While

Sean showed Garrett around, Amber and Andrea pulled out the tulle and pastel ribbon to make pew bows for Maya Brewer's wedding.

As soon as it was 9:00 a.m., she was back on the phone with the insurance agent, pushing to get her van repaired quickly and to report the damage to the store window. Desperation set in when she lost another round with the insurance company to rush the van's repairs. The repair shop estimated it would take at least another two weeks to finish. She needed it in ten days. They weren't pleased to hear she had a second claim within one week, but agreed to get security reinstated in twenty-four hours.

Saying a silent prayer, Amber asked God to send her ideas on how to get this wedding cake to the mountain resort next weekend. She needed to make a huge impression on the wedding guests if she hoped to make her business a success. She had to get her name out there if she hoped to stay afloat until the summer wedding season. It would be a long, dry spell between Christmas and the Valentine's Day weddings. So far she had five weddings in the one week around the busy sweethearts' holiday. This wedding could guarantee that she wouldn't need to lay off any of her dedicated staff after the holidays.

Andrea pulled the cinnamon crispies from the parchment paper and set them on the racks to cool while Amber listened to CiCi's report about the third parking ticket she'd received while making deliveries. They hadn't had this problem since Amber had had the van painted. But now that the police couldn't identify their vehicles for deliveries, it was an issue. This time, the parking meter had expired and snow had covered the windshield where they had placed the hot pink sign inside on the dash.

"What about those magnetic signs? We could each put them on our cars when we're doing deliveries, plus it would give you advertising," CiCi suggested as they finished boxing up the remainder of the pastries to go to the coffee shop down at the university.

"I thought of that. The sign company is hoping to put our new signs up next week. Maybe they can give me an estimate on the automobile signs, too."

Before lunch, Amber decorated two cakes for early afternoon pickup and boxed them up.

They had a rush of college students before she had a chance to check the invoice of Thanksgiving decorations and started pricing them. CiCi rotated the sheet cakes for the week through the stacks to let them cool.

After lunch Garrett had gone to run errands and get his tire repaired. She'd seen more police officers stop in for coffee and cinnamon rolls than she'd seen all month. She didn't suppose that was a coincidence.

Amber's mind returned to the huge wedding. Even if she could transport the four-tiered cake in the car, there was just no way it would all fit. And she needed her staff here to keep the shop open.

It was an hour trip up the canyon to the mountain resort. They couldn't make more than one trip with all the last-minute decorating she had to do on the cake. Not to mention they were expecting another small storm to bring a few inches of snow to Fossil Creek. That could mean a foot or more at the resort.

Desperate for something to take her mind off everything that had happened, Amber moved the costume masks to the back rack, clearing space for turkeys, snowmen and Christmas decorations.

It was almost closing time when she looked out the front windows and saw Garrett. She dropped the small box of party favors on the floor.

"Are you okay?" CiCi asked, looking out the window. "Did we have another order to be picked up? Did we forget something?"

"The guy coming this way…" Amber mumbled, kneeling to put the plastic turkeys back into the box. "He's the one I ran into." She wasn't sure why she was explaining his real identity to CiCi. "He's going to be working here for a while. They seem to believe all these mishaps are related to each other."

"That hunk in the gray polo is a cop?"

She pushed the box onto the shelf and hurried to pick up the packages. "That's him."

"That's the guy you flipped over to his roof and spun like a top? You didn't tell me he was good-looking and built like Brad Pitt." CiCi quickly fanned herself. "Oh, my, girl, he doesn't look happy."

Amber groaned. "I hope that scowl doesn't mean more bad news. It's bad enough the mess I made of my own business. I sure didn't need to ruin someone else's career, too." She finished filling the box just as he walked into the shop.

"Did they find her?" Amber asked immediately, standing to face him.

He looked a little puzzled. "Find who?"

"The girl who was attacked," she said, feeling the draft from the open door blow stray hair from her ponytail into her face. "You don't look happy."

Garrett looked worried. "I just tried calling and no one answered."

She felt the temperature in the room go up. "The phone hasn't rung, has it, CiCi?" She realized the two hadn't met and quickly introdcued them.

"All afternoon?" he asked, clearly surprised.

"We had one or two earlier, but..." She nervously brushed a stray hair behind her ear. "Sometimes the wet weather knocks out the phones in these old buildings. I'll check with the neighbors, though."

He raised his hand to stop her. "I'm sorry, I guess I've come to expect the worst this week. I just went to get the tire fixed, and found out it wasn't just a nail that I'd picked up somewhere. Someone put a metal spike right in the middle of it so I couldn't miss it."

"I'm sorry about the tires, Garrett." She figured she could ask him more about whether it was related after CiCi had gone. "Do you have any idea who might have done it?"

He shook his head. "I'm sure there's a list of criminals who'd like to get back at me. Anyway, I really wondered if I could interest you in having dinner with me. That is, unless you already have plans."

Amber glanced at CiCi, then back to Garrett and felt her heart race. "Sure, dinner's good." She needed to give him her cell phone number in addition to the work number. Maybe this wouldn't have caught her so off guard. "CiCi, if you'll just get the last of the dishes soaking, you can go on home."

"I really wouldn't mind finishing up here first..." CiCi said hesitantly.

Amber felt a blush creep into her face. "Thanks for

offering, CiCi, but I'll be working late anyway. I'll see you tomorrow. You do have my cell number, don't you?"

CiCi nodded. "Tomorrow's another late morning, remember. I'll see you about nine, then, if you're sure…"

"Go ahead and put down six o'clock on your time sheet." While CiCi gathered her belongings, Amber tried to mentally prepare herself to face Garrett. She couldn't help thinking how odd it was that she had no hesitation spending time with a cop—with Garrett— when she'd disliked police officers for so long. He and his brother seemed totally different from the officers who had changed the course of her life.

Amber heard the back door close and instinctively followed. "I'll be right back." She ran into the kitchen, pulling her ponytail holder from her hair. She placed her hair band on the coat rack, and peered out the peephole.

After reassuring herself that CiCi had made it to her car okay and no one was lurking outside, Amber turned and ran right into Garrett.

He caught and held her for a moment. He smiled gently, sending her heart into a flutter. "Sorry I startled you. I figured I may as well make sure you've locked up after she left."

Amber looked into his eyes, felt the strength of his embrace and found herself wanting to stay there. "I'm not used to having…visitors after hours, I guess."

"That's good information to have." His smile broadened. "I did consider leaving a message, but didn't want to leave a personal message on the bakery phone.

I wasn't sure if you'd pick up the messages, or your employees."

"Oh, right," she said, her mind spinning.

"Is this new, or have you always checked on your employees when they leave?" Garrett paused, holding her firmly against him.

"I started making sure my employees make it to their cars okay when your brother and his partner told me the rapist was in this area. I appreciated the warning. And I get the feeling you're here to issue another one."

He let her loose and stepped back. "Nothing quite as definite, but the bad news is I talked with some of the other officers, and without going back through the files we were able to recall two police-impersonator calls recently. I have some concerns I'd like to discuss with you. See if you can remember anything more. Too many things are happening. Someone had to have seen you."

"You really think they're after me?"

He nodded, seeming a little uncomfortable. "Yeah, I do, Amber. Are you okay ordering in, or would you like to go out for a bite?"

She turned and walked away, glancing at her work clothes, which even on a bad day weren't too bad. The long apron she wore protected them pretty well. Under most circumstances she'd freshen up before going out for the evening. Not tonight. She didn't want Garrett to think she was taking advantage of his help, flirting to get out of a ticket, or that she wasn't cooperating with an investigation.

Still, she thought, if he'd meant this to be a real date, he should have let her know earlier, or at least suggested another night. She'd better assume this was an official call. "Takeout would be fine. The pub a few doors down has great food and we could see if their phones are out, too."

Garrett nodded. "That sounds great. There are a couple things I'd like to clarify first."

She looked at him expectantly. "Yes?"

"I'm here partially on official orders, but mostly because I want to be here, because I want to make sure you're safe."

"What?" She stared into his brooding gray eyes, wondering why the police were so concerned all of a sudden. "Why? What did you find out?"

Her smile disappeared, and he cocked his head to one side. "Not much, yet. I believe you…but from what I can tell…"

She stopped and stared at him. "What's happened?"

He hesitated. "I'm not here as a police officer, Amber."

"They didn't fire you because of me, did they?"

He shook his head. "No. I'm here with the chief's blessing."

She stared at him, suddenly suspicious. She examined his shirt, noting how tight the polo shirt fit his shoulders and chest, yet was baggy at his waist. His jeans weren't too snug that he couldn't be carrying a concealed weapon. "Are you on duty?"

"No," he said, his eyes holding hers captive. He held his hands in the air. "I'm still on mandatory leave. You should probably be aware that I do wear a weapon when off duty."

Amber felt a connection with him that went beyond explanation. It was as if he'd read her mind, first with whether this was official or personal, then the gun.

Still, Samantha Taylor's observations of Garrett were ever present in her mind. He was most likely leaving soon, and she had finally found someplace she wanted to stay. Thanks to the friend who had shown her that a life with Christ beside her was much more fulfilling than drinking and running wild, she now had a purpose.

She'd realized she could listen to God's plan and make the most of the gifts He'd given her. She'd made friends here that she wanted to keep. And she definitely didn't want her police record to keep haunting her. So why, then, would the police chief give Garrett Matthews his blessing to come over here?

Amber backed away and shook her head. "You're creeping me out, Garrett. What's happened to make the chief of police send you over here to be my bodyguard?"

NINE

Garrett stepped away, realizing he'd gone too far, told her too much. Or she'd read him too well. "I know you saw something, Amber. And the chief knows you saw something, but…"

She placed a hand on her hip and squared her shoulders. "But what?"

Her stare was right on target, hitting the bull's-eye, shattering his plan to bits. He couldn't lead her on. "Nothing has turned up. They found no evidence of any kind of scuffle."

She turned and walked to the front lobby door. "I don't have time for this."

Garrett looked stunned. "Wait, can I at least explain?" He paused, waiting for her to argue. "They believe you. *We* believe you, that is. It's just that there's still more questions we need answered about the kidnapping. The chief hoped I could talk through it with you again and find a lead."

Amber looked tired and skeptical. "I've told you everything I know. I've been in to try to talk to the police every day…they've never asked any more questions." She didn't need to tell him it had been mostly to try to see him again. "No one is willing to even talk to me, Garrett. Most of them treated me as if I'd killed you," she said in a fragile voice.

"Oh, no, if you'd killed me, you'd never see the end of them," he joked.

She unlocked the door and motioned for him to leave. "I don't need to cause you, or me, any more trouble, Officer. So just go…."

The smart Aleck in him had apparently shown up at the wrong time. Again. He pushed the door closed, bringing him face-to-face with her. "Trust me, Amber. I'm here to help you. I'm as disappointed as you are that no one's asked you more questions, but trust me I plan to ask a lot more until we find out what's happening." His gaze held her captive.

"I don't blame you, Garrett. You were hurt. But they didn't even talk to any of the businesses in the area."

"How do you know that?"

"Because I asked!" she blurted out in frustration. "They didn't even know anything about what had happened Thursday night," she rambled on. "The girl is probably dead by now. If I'd just backed up into him…" She let out a heavy sigh of responsibility.

Garrett took her hand and pulled her into his arms. "Hey, don't do this to yourself."

She shook her head. "Don't be nice, Garrett. I ran into you. You're hurt and it's all my fault."

"Accidents happen, and I'm not hurt that bad. Just a twinge now and then, see?" He raised his arm and moved his head from side to side, hoping the pain stayed away. "I can think of easier ways to meet a beautiful woman, but they aren't nearly as interesting."

Her lips twitched. "I don't date cops. I don't even like cops."

"That's okay, I don't like sweets, so we're even."

She looked at him and the moisture in her eyes gave way to laughter. "So why are you really here, then, if it's not to find the girl, and it's not to feed your sweet tooth?"

The silence in the room turned deafening, and Garrett wasn't sure how to answer her. He wished Chief Thomas had never issued the order to keep her out of the way.

"Give me a chance to figure this out, Amber, before the suspect can target you, too. I'm not giving up on this case until I have answers. But first and foremost, I don't want to let you down. I want to change your mind about cops. One cop, anyway."

Amber lowered her long eyelashes. "You don't have to do that," she said softly.

He waited a few minutes for her to argue. "Maybe I want to. I don't want you hurt. So, are we still on for dinner?"

She opened her eyes and looked into his with a skeptical smile. "I don't understand why you think I'm in danger."

"Gangs have tagged the area heavily this week. Not that it has anything to do with you personally, until that rock came through your front window anyway. The downtown area has been one of their favorite hangouts for a while now, as you've probably noticed. The Old Town Association has put a lot of pressure on the mayor.... In any case I'd rather not take the chance. And if we work together to find this guy before he can strike again, he won't have another opportunity to threaten anyone...mostly you." He leaned his head closer, waiting for her to meet him halfway. "Yes?"

Garrett couldn't out-and-out lie to her. He cared too much about Amber to do that. He couldn't explain it, not to the chief, and especially not to her. He couldn't understand what had happened the night of their accident. His life seemed to have changed in that split second. He knew the outcome of this one assignment could end his career and nix any hopes he had of moving up to a federal agency. He hoped it was worth the risk, personally and professionally.

She nodded and stepped closer into his arms.

He'd never thought much about why he was never able to find the right woman to settle down with. He was determined to break away from the stereotypical youngest-child syndrome, even though his adopted sister, Kira had officially knocked him out of the position. Through school, he'd been the class clown. The one they didn't expect to go far. The one least likely to have a steady girlfriend. He'd pushed hard to break away from the low expectations.

In the process of proving himself, he'd forgotten to live, laugh or love. Amber Scott made him want to do all three.

"One more thing that might make you feel more comfortable. I've asked my brother and his fiancée to stop by...to go through it with us."

Suddenly he felt as if he could make a difference right here in his hometown. Even though his life hadn't flashed in front of his eyes, even though he'd come nowhere near dying, it seemed like he'd been given another chance to find God's plan for his life. And running from everything he'd known seemed like the biggest mistake he could make.

She wrapped her arms around his waist. "Just so you know up front, Garrett, I'm not the girl that you're looking for." Her hand was an inch from his gun.

He backed away from her. "And how would you know who I'm looking for?"

"I don't think that's part of your investigation, is it?" Amber watched as he studied her. "So, now that we have that cleared up, let's order dinner."

Amber hoped to get a better idea of whether Garrett was serious about finding the missing girl, or if this was all just a game he was playing.

And maybe by the time they'd finished eating, she'd be able to put up the shield to protect her from her own weakness—charming men.

"So should we order food for Nick and..."

"Sarah. Sure, I'll pick out something for my brother. You can choose a meal for Sarah."

"I don't even know Sarah."

"Yes, you do. She's the one who rented the chicken costume from you for the Harvest Festival last month. The short, dark-haired officer..."

"His partner?" She stepped back. "He really is engaged to his trainee? I thought that was just a rumor," she said almost to herself.

"Who have you been talking to?"

She didn't reply immediately, realizing that if she told on Samantha Taylor, he'd probably figure out why she thought she wasn't his type, too.

"Amber, who told you about their engagement, besides me, I mean?"

"I plead the Fifth," she said, flashing him an innocent smile.

"I'll let you get away with that for now, since they'll be here soon," Garrett said as he studied her. "But be forewarned, if it's going to come up eventually."

"Why don't we run down to check on the phones and order dinner? Then I'll come back and clear a place for us to eat." Amber lifted the phone to check the connection. "Nothing. I sure hope it's not just my line." She put her coat on and joined Garrett.

Half an hour later, Amber greeted Sarah Roberts while Garrett was gone to pick up the meals. "Hi, it's good to see you again," Amber said.

Sarah looked around the shop. "You, too. You've been busy in here, and it looks like your hard work is paying off."

"It's been going really well. I'm just busy enough through the holidays, and then I'm expecting a lull. People are kind of tired of sugar after the holidays."

"True," Sarah said, roaming the costumes. "I've been meaning to call and see if you have time to do a little cake New Year's Eve, for a small, quiet celebration."

Amber wasn't sure how serious Sarah was. If it was for a wedding, she was getting an awfully late start. "Sure, what do you have in mind?"

"I'll call you later to discuss the details. I'm not sure of everything yet. How're you doing after the incident the other night?"

Amber pushed the racks toward the window to give them an extra thick curtain of privacy. "I'm getting along okay."

"If you ever feel you need to get away from here, let me know. Sometimes it's easier to be around other people. My sister and I have an extra room." Sarah kept up the conversation as if they were long lost friends. "So, how many cop costumes have you rented out?" she asked.

Garrett walked in the shop with two sacks of food just as Sarah asked the question.

"I looked that up the next day, just to be sure I was ready in case a detective asked, but it's been three days and so far, no one has contacted me to verify anything about the incident."

"I understand your frustration," Sarah said sympathetically.

She pointed to the costume racks. "I bought a dozen police costumes because they were so much less expensive to buy that many. They were on back order for a couple of weeks and didn't get in until the twenty-fifth, so most of the interested customers had to go elsewhere. I did rent out three, but they were all to men from the senior home," she answered, "so it couldn't have been them."

"That would have been too easy if he'd rented the costume from you, wouldn't it?" Sarah said sarcastically.

Garrett set the takeout food on the table. "Has anyone talked to Nick?"

"Estimated time of arrival five minutes," Sarah said.

Garrett walked over to the costumes and quickly thumbed through them.

Amber smiled at him. "Shopping?"

"I thought you said the cop costumes were popular,"

Garrett responded. He joined the women at the table, waiting for Amber's answer.

"I had at least a dozen other calls before I even started carrying costumes, which is why I bought so many. I've been tempted to take them off the racks completely after this."

Nick arrived right on time. "Hi, Amber, Garrett." He turned to Sarah and his face lit up as he pulled Sarah into his arms and kissed her. "Hi, how was your day?"

"Productive," Sarah answered with a smile. She was clearly in love. "I have a new lead to follow, so that'll give me something to use for training. There's just nothing as motivating as the real deal."

Amber felt like she was spying on them as she set out paper plates and flatware and asked what everyone wanted to drink.

Sarah followed her to the kitchen to fill the orders while Nick went to wash up.

When they were all seated Nick said a blessing. As they started to eat, Garrett wasted no time in explaining why he had asked Sarah and Nick to join them. "I've been thinking about the guy you saw. You think he stabbed her because you didn't hear a gun, right?"

"I don't remember hearing anything, but he had something sticking into her back because she arched away from him. When Lieutenant Chavez and Officer Taylor searched the scene, they didn't see any sign of blood or an altercation at all, so I don't know. After all of this time, I'm beginning to wonder if…"

"Don't go there," Nick warned. "I can understand why you might be tempted. It's discouraging and frightening…."

"It wasn't your imagination, Amber," Garrett finished for his brother.

"But you said there was no evidence. Except the yellow SUV. It was still there," she said.

"It still is, same spot. I'm going to see what I can find out about it," Garrett said.

"Be careful, Garrett," Sarah cautioned. "Maybe Kent and I should do some digging, keep you two out of more trouble."

"Who's Kent?" Amber asked.

Nick took a drink and sat down. "Our other brother, he's an undercover narcotics officer."

"You're all cops?" Amber said, arching her eyebrows.

Nick laughed. "Our dad's a retired one."

"I figured as much. He's so much like the two of you. Is your sister a police officer, too?" Amber asked of no one in particular.

"No," Garrett said quickly.

Nick and Sarah looked at Garrett with an odd expression on their faces. "So Amber, tell us what you recall."

She let out a deep breath. "I didn't hear a gun pop, unless he used a silencer. I don't know," she said, feeling insecure. They all knew far more about crime scenes than she did.

"What about this sound?" Nick asked.

Suddenly an electric buzzing noise sounded, and she jumped. "What is that?"

Nick held up a gun. "A taser. Sometimes referred to as a stun gun."

"You think he used one on the victim?"

Garrett nodded. "Maybe. Sarah's the one that mentioned it, actually. Did you hear a noise like that?"

She shrugged. "No, I don't recall…." She wasn't liking this conversation.

"It may not be quite as loud outside or when it's pressed against the body," Garrett said. "Plus, traffic and trees may have muffled some of the sound. In here it's just echoing off the walls." He must have seen the fear in her expression. "It's okay, we're not going to hurt you."

Nick held it up and studied it. "Do you happen to have a computer, we could show you some videos of idiots…"

"No," she said abruptly. "Why?"

"We could show you demonstrations of their use," Sarah corrected.

Nick shrugged. "I was thinking of the college kids who video it for laughs. Crazy kids…."

Sarah rolled her eyes. "Tasers have become pretty well known lately, and though the police have strict rules around them, use and sales by the general public are pretty much unregulated. But if someone wants to really disable someone, there are some pretty powerful units available that will allow them to do it." Sarah let out a breath, as if struggling to tell of her own experience on the victim's side of a taser.

Nick took hold of Sarah's hand. "Sarah was tased by the rapist we were looking for at the Harvest Festival. She insisted on putting herself in the line of fire, and he took the bait."

"That's terrible," Amber said with a look of concern.

"When I was tased in training, it wasn't pleasant, but when it was over, I was okay. The one the attacker used on me was set higher and for longer. I couldn't fight back. I dropped to the ground like I was dead. For what seemed like forever, I thought I was."

Amber stared at the gun that Nick had set on the table across from her. "And you want to try that out on one of us?" She cut her food but nothing looked appetizing right now.

"No," Garrett insisted. "I thought Sarah and Nick might be able to explain their experience with them. While I've qualified to use it, and had to be shocked with it, what we do in training is nothing compared to how it feels when they are misused. I don't plan to actually shock anyone. You're sure you didn't hear anything that sounded like that?"

She let out a sigh of relief. "But surely I would remember hearing something, wouldn't I?"

"Stress could be a factor. Noise of the traffic, everything... We were outside an apartment complex when the guy used it on Sarah, and we could barely hear it, but it was bouncing off the buildings, and we heard their voices more than anything."

"And you couldn't stop him?" Amber said, appalled that anyone would let someone they cared about go through that.

Sarah looked at her. "Of course they stopped him. I was wired, but this guy had caused interference in our audio connection. He dragged me away before the team realized I was back. Even with him using the highest power available, I'm okay. So maybe the woman you saw is, too."

She nodded. "I hope so. It's been days. I can't believe no one has been reported missing yet."

"You know how college kids can be," Garrett said. "They don't stop to think that someone could be hurt. And when they do call someone in missing, it usually turns out they were just staying with a friend for a few days and didn't think it was important to tell anyone. Friends sometimes don't want to get a class-mate in trouble."

She thought back to her rebellious years. After her arrest, she'd been too embarrassed to contact any of her roommates. "Yeah, I guess I remember how it was. That's why I can't believe the police won't make a public announcement. If the students hear someone saw something that concerns them, maybe they wouldn't be afraid to speak up."

Nick looked at her with concern. "You can't bring attention to yourself, Amber. It's not safe."

"Nick is right," Sarah agreed.

"We don't want to take the chance of antagonizing the suspect right now," Garrett said, his gaze sincere. "Right now, it appears he has no idea you witnessed his abduction. Who knows what he'd do if he realizes you saw him?"

TEN

Amber felt a chill go up her spine at the thought of the assailant coming after her. "I hadn't even considered that."

Garrett's smile of sympathy softened her anger toward the police. At the same time, it made her realize how foolish she'd been.

"Nick needs to get back on duty soon, so let's go through what happened. Could you describe the scene again? Let's say the front door here is where the cars were parked. It's a lot closer probably, but is that about right?"

Amber nodded, barely able to think after the fear he'd put into her. She looked around, trying to place everything at the scene. Talking it through, she moved tables and showed Sarah and Nick about where she would have been standing.

Garrett started the scenario. "So, you're the victim in the SUV, you shake your head no, and he yanks the door open and pulls you out." He pretended to open the door and pulled Amber to her feet. "Then what?"

"He pulled her to the car, which was parked behind the SUV. He leaned close and said something to her."

"You didn't hear anything that was said?" He

pushed her hair out of his way. "Was her hair in a ponytail? If her hair was in his face, and you didn't hear anything, how'd you know he'd said something?"

"Yeah, it was. I saw." She grabbed a rubber band from the supply she kept downstairs and put her hair up into a loose ponytail, talking as she went back to her position in Garrett's grasp. "That was kind of why I wasn't terribly sure at that point that it was anything serious. At first, it looked a little romantic, but then she kept kind of jerking away, and he looked like he was saying something again. Then the guy pulled out a pair of handcuffs and struggled to put them on her."

Garrett reached out and borrowed a pair of cuffs from Nick. "Did he look like he knew what he was doing, or was he fumbling with the cuffs?"

"Kind of fumbling, I guess, but she was starting to struggle. It looked like she knocked them out of his hand, or maybe he was juggling a gun or something and the handcuffs." Amber felt her skin flush, recalling the night she'd run from the police. "He got one cuff on her left hand," she said, waiting as Garrett put one on her left wrist. "He didn't hold them like that," she said. "He opened the cuff and held it at the hinge, holding them open."

Garrett froze, drawing his brows to a V. "I've seen someone do that. Who was it?" He looked to Nick.

"I've never seen that technique. It doesn't seem like they'd make it through the academy if they can't cuff someone cleaner than that." Nick shook his head.

Sarah watched, silently waiting for Amber's next instruction.

She took a deep breath and closed her eyes for a few

seconds, thinking of how the girl had gotten loose. "Try to grab my other hand."

Four times Amber tried to get away and failed. Garrett would have had her cuffed in a few seconds. Her feeble attempts at getting away left them all laughing.

"Did she elbow him, or kick him at all?" Sarah suggested.

Amber laughed. "I don't know, but I'm obviously doing something wrong." She turned and looked into Garrett's eyes. "So we need to assume he wasn't as proficient as you are. Or I'm wimpier than she was. Either way, would you please pretend I get the one hand free," she said with another laugh, unable to erase her smile as his gaze made her heart skip a beat.

Without a word, Garrett let her hand slip from his.

"This guy couldn't have made it into any law enforcement job around here. No one would make it through the academy if they can't even manage to cuff a woman…. Unless she's had professional training," Nick said, smiling at Sarah.

She laughed. The teasing gaze between them was clearly love, and Amber was still stunned to realize that this was the pair that had met only a few months earlier.

"Okay, moving along," Garrett said as Amber spun around, trying to pull her cuffed hand from his clasp and pretending to beat him with her free hand.

"Did she have anything in her hand?" Sarah asked.

Amber kept pretending to struggle with Garrett. "It sure seems like she had something, but it had to have been small, because it wasn't holding her back." She playfully hit him again.

"Okay, then what?"

"The girl went to hit him again and missed. He pushed her against the car, and they struggled. She was pulling and pushing him, but he finally got the other cuff on her."

Garrett looked around then quickly walked her to the bakery cases and pressed her against the curved glass. "That will work as a car. Are they on the driver's side or the passenger's side?"

"Passenger's."

"So pretend this is the front of the car, and to the left is the trunk, then how'd she push him around if he had her pressed against the car?"

Amber dreaded acting this part out. "Ummm, he body-slammed her, then reached around and yanked her arm back. It looked painful. She slid to the left," she said, sidestepping. "Once she was away from the roof of the car and the windows, he fastened the cuffs and pulled her away from the car. This all happened really fast."

Without the body slam, Garrett pressed her against the glass again, and followed her lead with the struggle. "Did he put her in the passenger's side, or behind the driver?"

"This side. And now he got the cuff on her right hand and yanked her away from the car, and she made a noise, not really a scream, but something." She paused the action while Garrett gently fastened the other cuff and helped her stand up.

"Sorry to interrupt but it seems strange that all this time, she didn't yell or anything," Sarah said.

Amber's voice quivered, and it was tough to keep going. "I heard a slight protest, more like she was asking the cop what she'd done, when she first got out of the SUV, right before he whispered in her ear, but that was it until this point. I never heard her scream." She felt her voice dissolve and silence spread through the room.

Amber heard the hushed sound of Nick's police radio and a filmstrip of memories flashed in her mind.

She'd gone over the kidnapping so many times in her mind the past few days, why was it so difficult this time? She took another deep breath, let it out and tried to block the memories of her arrest so long ago. She couldn't believe it was so fresh in her memory tonight.

"We're almost finished, Amber. You can do it." The deep timbre of Garrett's voice brought her back to the kidnapping and the frightened girl that occupied her thoughts.

She nodded silently. "He covered her mouth…and body-slammed her against the car again so he could open the door."

Garrett put one hand over her mouth and touched her back with the other. She leaned against the glass again while he pretended to open the car door. "Door's open," Garrett said quietly.

Amber took a deep breath, struggling with the memories of the incident and the guilt that she could have backed her van into his car and changed the course of everything that night. With a shaky voice she said, "That's when he took a step back and yanked her away from the car…" Her voice faded away. "And then she arched her back, like she was in dire pain. I heard some muffled sounds, agonized like… The girl collapsed, and he shoved her into the car."

Amber was drained, just thinking about it.

She stood back upright and turned her back to Garrett so he could take the cuffs off. He quickly unlocked them, then handed them back to Nick.

"Are you okay?" he said quietly, wrapping his warm hands around her wrists. Acting it out brought back the memories of not only witnessing the incident, but being the victim of a real arrest. Tears threatened to flow.

She nodded silently, and Garrett pulled her into his embrace.

"I'm sorry to put you through that again, Amber. You did great," he whispered into her neck.

She buried her face against his strong chest and hugged him, welcoming his comfort. Her heart raced. Her breathing was uneven.

"You did the right thing," he said, patting her back. "I'm glad it wasn't you," he whispered into her ear, holding her close.

After a few minutes of silence, Sarah broke the awkward silence. "I guess the only thing left to figure out is if you could have heard a taser or stun gun. The one that the guy used on me knocked me to the ground, so it might have made her collapse, too. Did the victim look tense as she fell limp, or did she look relaxed?"

When she didn't respond, Garrett pushed her away and said her name again, softly. "Amber?"

She blinked the moisture from her eyes, nodded to him, then moved to the table again, sitting next to Sarah. "I hadn't thought about it, really."

"When tased, the body is jerkier, the muscles tense from the electrocution. Sometimes stocky men go

An Important Message from the Editors of Steeple Hill Books

Dear Reader,

Because you've chosen to read one of our fine Love Inspired® Suspense novels, we'd like to say "thank you!" And, as a **special** way to thank you, we've selected <u>two more</u> of the books you love so well, **and** two surprise gifts to send you — absolutely **FREE!**

Please enjoy them with our compliments...

Jean Gordon

Editor,
Love Inspired
Suspense

Peel off seal and place inside...

HOW TO VALIDATE YOUR
EDITOR'S FREE GIFTS!
"THANK YOU"

1 Peel off the FREE GIFTS SEAL from front cover. Place it in the space provided at right. This automatically entitles you to receive two free books and two exciting surprise gifts.

2 Send back this card and you'll get 2 Love Inspired® Suspense books. These books are worth over $10, but are yours absolutely FREE!

3 There's no catch. You're under no obligation to buy anything. We charge nothing—ZERO—for your first shipment. And you don't have to make any minimum number of purchases—not even one!

4 We call this line Love Inspired Suspense because each month you'll receive books that are filled with riveting inspirational suspense. These tales of intrigue and romance feature Christian characters facing challenges to their faith and to their lives! You'll like the convenience of getting them delivered to your home well before they are in stores. And you'll love our discount prices, too!

5 We hope that after receiving your free books you'll want to remain a subscriber. But the choice is yours—to continue or cancel, anytime at all! So why not take us up on our invitation, with no risk of any kind. You'll be glad you did!

6 And remember... just for validating your Editor's Free Gifts Offer, we'll send you 2 books and 2 gifts, *ABSOLUTELY FREE!*

YOURS FREE!

We'll send you two fabulous surprise gifts (worth about $10) absolutely FREE, simply for accepting our no-risk offer!

rigid and collapse when they're tased. When someone faints, the body is more relaxed. It just shuts down, so to speak. Since no blood was found, one of these two is most likely to have happened."

"She was tense," she said. Amber looked at Sarah and smiled. "You don't think I made this up?"

"Not at all. And for the record, I think those who do are few and far between, Amber. I'm new to the department, so I won't pretend to know all of the nuances here, but it's my guess this is being hushed by politics."

Nick nodded silently, and glanced first to Sarah, then to Amber. "Amber, I can assure you that none of us here are questioning what you saw and we'll do all that we can to locate this girl. We all figured it was being handled by the detectives, or we would have stayed on it."

She couldn't believe she'd created such a mess and no one believed her. Why? Did they just look at her history and decide she was making things up?

Nick stood, pushing the chair on the linoleum floor. "I need to get back to work, but if you need anything, let me know."

Amber felt the tears threaten again. "I can't thank you guys enough for all you've done. I keep asking God why this happened. But what confuses me even more is how I was lucky enough to run into someone so understanding. All of you."

Garrett had a look in his eyes that alarmed her. "I'm beginning to think luck had nothing to do with it, Amber. I'm afraid God's been working on this for a long while."

Amber wasn't sure how to respond.

Nick and Sarah must have felt the emotions change,

as well, because they thanked them for dinner and quickly said their goodbyes.

She waited for the door to close behind the couple, then locked it and looked at Garrett. "Would you care to elaborate on that theory of yours?"

ELEVEN

Garrett couldn't understand what had happened to him. He'd never been one to fall for girls who spent more time worried about their looks than their studies, but come to think of it, there hadn't been more than one or two that had ever held his interest like Amber Scott. Her blatant faith and determination to do the right thing was an irresistible temptation, despite her striking good looks.

She looked at him and waited.

Lord, I don't know what to tell her. This isn't just about the lack of an investigation or why the chief ordered me to keep an eye on her, it's all about what You have placed on my heart. How do I tell her that You are totally in control here? That we are both totally in Your hands.

"I appreciate the time you took tonight to make it look like the police are doing something on the investigation, Garrett…." She walked to the kitchen and pulled out a bin of flour. "But I have a lot…"

"I know you do," he interrupted, his voice barely a murmur. He followed, dodging her as she moved from one shelf to another, pulling huge stainless bowls and canisters and measuring pitchers across the room. Then she started dumping ingredients into the huge mixer that looked like it was older than both of them. "It's not an act, Amber. I don't know quite how to explain it to you."

Amber put an eight-cup glass measuring cup of milk into the microwave and hit start. "Try," she said with a look that he'd guess was more fear than smile.

Garrett crossed his arms over his chest and leaned against the counter. "Are you sure you really want to know?"

"What's that supposed to mean?" She cracked eggs into a bowl, added oil and glanced at the microwave as if she was waiting for the hot milk.

"You don't like cops," he suggested.

She looked at him through narrowed eyes. "So?"

"I get the feeling that there's more than just a professional bond between you and me." He cleared his throat. "Or that there could be. Except for this hang-up you have with the police…"

Amber quickly looked away.

He reworded the question in friendlier terms. "Any chance of changing that?"

"You already have," she said. "At least toward a few of you. I didn't like Lieutenant Chavez. And Samantha Taylor…I'm not too sure about her."

"Sam's okay," he said flippantly.

Amber's smile faded as she stared at him. "I think she has a thing for you…" she said, glancing up to see his reaction.

"I think you misunderstood."

She shrugged as if she were trying not to care. "Maybe...."

He wasn't even listening. He didn't want to think about anyone but her right now. *Help her realize I don't say this lightly, God.* "I have a thing for you, Amber."

They looked at each other and smiled broadly, his honesty disarming them. He took a step toward Amber and she toward him just as there was a loud knock on the alley entrance.

Amber startled.

"Are you expecting anyone?" he asked, holding her back as he moved toward the door.

"No," she said, "Maybe it's CiCi...."

Garrett looked out. "It's Samantha."

Officer Samantha Taylor knocked again, then Amber heard the antique doorbell ring up in the apartment.

Amber moved to open the door as Garrett went to the front lobby, motioning for her to keep his presence quiet.

Samantha reminded her of their meeting after the accident. "I was off for a couple of days, but I wanted to stop in and see how you're doing."

"Fine. Thanks for thinking of me," Amber said, hesitating to move away from the door.

"Good. Would you and Garrett mind if I came in for a minute?"

"Would we...?" Amber's voice faded away.

Samantha Taylor smiled. "I noticed his Mustang out front. I presumed he was here. Maybe he's down the block at the pub, though that's not like him."

Amber froze.

"What's up, Sam?" Garrett said as he joined them.

Sam tried to step inside, but Amber was in the way. Garrett took hold of Amber's arm and pulled her toward him, allowing Samantha to come inside.

Sam closed the door and smiled. "I'm a little puzzled about the investigation of the police impersonator case."

"They *are* investigating? Who's working it?" Garrett asked.

"That's what I'm wondering. What do you know about it?" She pulled a notepad from her chest pocket. "I noticed that the SUV is still in the same parking place that it was when the crime took place, so I asked your brother about it. He said you might be here."

Amber crossed her arms over her chest and watched silently. He couldn't help but wonder how Samantha would interpret Amber's body language. It might be wishful thinking, but Garrett wanted to believe she was jealous.

"I don't know anything about it. I'm still on mandatory leave." Garrett glanced at the beautiful party planner. Were his feelings for her obvious to anyone else? "I wanted to be sure Ms. Scott was doing okay."

Samantha smiled, and Garrett knew she understood not to ask. Garrett and Sam had gone through the academy together, so they'd already built a high level of trust, and he knew Samantha was head over heels in love with her husband. Sam turned to Amber. "I hope we can find this guy and ease all our minds."

He couldn't imagine what had been said to give Amber the impression that Sam was interested in him.

They were like brother and sister. "I know you gave Amber a ride home that night, but it sounds like you were at the crime scene, too, right?"

"Yeah, good old Lieutenant Chavez asked me to go with him and Ms. Scott to the scene. There was plenty to check on, but Chavez didn't think it was relevant. I tried to talk to Nick, but…with the investigation he went through, I'm guessing he doesn't want to push the envelope quite yet. He suggested I talk to you before going to the chief. What's going on, Garrett?"

"I'm not sure, but something's not right. That's one reason I'm here, to see if Amber has recalled anything else that might open up a lead in the case. I wish I could get hold of the full report," Garrett said, trying to avoid looking at Amber. "So what did you see that gives you reason to think they should have pushed…"

"I'm not sure it's enough to call the lieutenant on, but I'm pretty sure that there's enough to investigate Amber's report." She pressed her finger to her earpiece and handed him a sheet of paper with her notes. "I've got to go. You have my cell number if you have questions," she said. "If you think I need to take it to someone else, let me know."

By the time Garrett had read all her notes, Samantha Taylor was gone. She'd been asked to run the plates on the yellow SUV the night of the incident. Even though she'd given the lieutenant the name of the owner, he'd almost bet it wasn't mentioned in the lieutenant's report.

He turned the page. The car was registered to Marcus Smith. According to her incident report, no one had even suggested contacting him.

The anger in Amber's voice caught his attention immediately. "What did she mean by she *thinks* there's enough to investigate? Why didn't you tell me everyone has totally blown it off as lies?" She stomped to the front door and opened it.

"Because we didn't," he argued, pushing the door out of her hand and closing it tight. "Why do you think I'm here? And Nick and Sarah and Samantha? We've all told you directly that we believe you…." He studied her, wondering if he was imagining a tremor on her lower lip. "So why are you acting so guilty?"

He hadn't been on the receiving side of a woman's lethal stare since he'd moved away to college…and that woman had been his mother.

"Because every officer who responded that night made it perfectly clear, Garrett. I am guilty."

"It was an accident."

"You shouldn't be here, Garrett. Let yourself out." She pivoted on her heel and stomped back to the security of the kitchen.

Garrett paused, closing his eyes and saying a quick prayer before taking off to find her. Before he got to the kitchen he heard a door close at the top of the stairs to her apartment. He waited a few minutes, mentally sorting everything out.

Why didn't she believe him? Could she really think that he'd lie to her? That all of them would?

He looked around the shop and replayed the evening. She claimed she didn't like cops, yet he'd seen no indication of that until after Sam had arrived. Maybe it was something Sam had told Amber that night.

Or maybe she'd read between the lines and knew the chief had sent him to keep her quiet. He needed to come clean, tell her that the chief couldn't be upset that he'd come here, that he'd sent him…. He couldn't tell her that. He wasn't here to keep her quiet. He was here to keep her safe.

Garrett stomped up the stairs and knocked. "Amber, I'm not leaving without you. And besides, even if I wanted to, I can't leave until you're down here to lock the door behind me."

She finally opened the door, a look of frustration and fear on her face, "I'm sorry, Garrett, I know it's not your fault that they aren't investigating, but it's so…" She paused, letting her voice fade away as she shook her head.

"Wrong," he suggested. "The police can't expect the community to have faith in us when one person brushes things under the rug. I know." He peeked into her apartment, wondering if it was still her grandmother's decor, or if she'd taken time to put her own touches in it. "I wish I could explain all of this to you, Amber…but unfortunately, I can't understand what's going on, either. I need some time to look into it. Trust me."

Her eyes darted to him, then she quickly looked away. "I'm going to have to call it a night. I appreciate your family's hospitality, but I miss my own place."

"Sure," he replied, turning around on the small landing and heading down the steep steps. "Since I sent CiCi away before she could finish dishes, could I help you do them before we leave?" He had to clear the air now, before she believed his feelings for her were fabricated, too. "I feel like I owe you that."

She hesitated. "Well, I still have a lot to do to get ready for the wedding this weekend, and I'm running the shop with a small staff so it's been really nice to have your help. We're all putting in long hours. You don't have to, but it would be nice to start the morning with a clean kitchen. Thanks."

Garrett turned to face her, hoping she meant that personally, not professionally. "It gives us a little more time to talk."

A tentative smile softened the seriousness that had dampened the mood after Sam's visit. "I'm sorry I ran off, Garrett." She took one more step down the stairs, "I'd like to spend more time with you, but I'm having a tough time sorting through the crime and the accident and my interest in you. And whether you should really be here at all. Personally, I mean."

"It is a bit complicated," he admitted. "I want to assure you that I'm going to keep looking for this girl, but I hold no ill feelings about the accident. It's been a mixed blessing, running into each other. I don't much like being off duty, but I can't deny I don't mind that we met—however God had to do it."

Even in the dim overhead light he could see her blush. "Maybe we could plan to do something, a movie, or…"

"You busy tomorrow night?" He leaned closer and paused, wondering if she could hear his heart beating half as clearly as he could. If he couldn't control his reaction better than this over a woman, he'd better take sniper off his list of career goals.

Amber rested her hands on his shoulders and smiled. "Maybe we should wait till the investigation is over?"

He looked into her eyes, hoping he was reading her correctly. "I was going to ask what investigation? But you might take me seriously."

"You have a warped sense of humor," she whispered.

"Goes with the territory," he said, easing her closer. "I liked your hair down tonight, during dinner. I don't think I've seen it down before. Even the night of the accident, you wore it up."

"Health Department regulations. Most days I forget to take it down." She reached up and pulled the band from her head and let the hair tumble over his hands as he gently touched her chin and drew her face to his.

He wasn't sure how long they stood there on the stairs, kissing, but this time it was his cell phone ringing that ended it. He wanted to ignore it, but he figured it was wise for them to slow things down. He took a deep breath and answered, admiring the look of contentment on Amber's face. She walked past him to the kitchen, trying to act as if nothing had happened.

Garrett followed, trying to get a better connection in the old building.

She drained the dirty water from the sink and started fresh, hot soapy water in the opposite side. As soon as she'd finger combed her hair off her face, she tied it up again.

"What did you say?" he asked Nick, trying to focus on his brother's voice instead of the racing of his heart.

"I asked if you're still at Amber's."

"Yeah, why?"

"There's rumors that the Scorpions and the Snakes

are going to face off downtown. I'd suggest you stay put for a while, for your protection, and to make sure Amber's safe."

"Okay. Thanks for the warning. Be careful, and call if you need anything."

He checked his gun and made his way through the kitchen. "That was Nick. There's some trouble brewing downtown." He made a note to start bringing his Kevlar vest home with him.

Amber watched as he tucked his Glock back into his holster, and turned away. "Is it really that bad? I mean, that they'd call you to help."

"No, they're taking care of it. Nick suggested we stick around for a while. So why don't we lock the front door and then you can let me help wash dishes." He went to the front window and looked out, seeing little activity except a few stragglers leaving the pub.

"Have they found any leads to who put the rock through my window?" Amber said, following him with the keys for the deadbolt.

"The gang task force is getting a handle on it. I'm still hoping your window was caught in the crossfire of a gang fight. It's not like the gangs of L.A., but it's definitely a concern for Fossil Creek. This used to be quiet farming community. But when the police have to make an arrest at the Harvest Festival, with families all around, we all get a little concerned."

"Yeah, I was there. It was pretty strange to watch Nick and Sarah in action that night. Were you down here that night, too?"

He nodded. "I know this was your grandmother's shop, but surely there's a safer area of town you could move the business to and find an apartment some-where."

"I can't afford to relocate," she said, pulling the tables and costume racks back to where they were when he'd arrived.

"Is business going okay?"

She nodded. "Foot traffic is slower than it was back in Nana's day, with conscientious people like you who are cutting back on their sweets," she said with a smile.

"Have you looked in the mirror recently? You ob-viously don't eat much of your own baking," he teased back.

"I have my days, but I get tired of the sweets, too. That's why I decided to combine the party planning with the bakery and whole party store idea. Most people are cutting back on sugar, but they are more interested in throwing elaborate parties. And for those who don't have time, I'm here to help with the planning. I learned a few things from my business classes before I dropped out of college. Find something people want, that they don't have time to do themselves, and give it a unique twist." She spun around and looked at him. "Now, the bakery is only a small portion of my business, and the party planning is taking a bigger bite out of the pie. So, one day, I hope to spend less hours baking at 3:00 a.m. and more hours coordinating celebrations. Speaking of which, Sarah mentioned needing to talk to me about doing something for her on New Year's Eve. Are they…?"

"I'm not sure when the big day is," he said with a shrug. "I know you have work to get done." He headed for the kitchen just as they heard angry voices outside. Garrett didn't like the sounds of them.

Garrett pulled his weapon and headed to the front of the shop to look out the window. "You stay right there," he ordered.

Just as he walked into the front lobby, he heard gunfire in the alley and spun around.

"Get upstairs into your apartment, Amber."

She grabbed his arm as he hurried to the back door and followed as he continued into the back entryway. "Don't go out there, Garrett."

He pulled out his cell phone and called Nick, concerned when he didn't answer. "Don't worry, I'm not crazy enough to go out there without my gear. I'm going to make sure you go up the stairs into your apartment." He heard sirens in the distance and said a silent prayer for the responding officers.

She ran up the stairs and they both rushed inside.

"Leave the lights off and lead me to the window."

She took his hand and directed him across the room, around a coffee table and onto the sofa. "Let me open the shade a little."

"I'd rather you not." He looked out, seeing two squad cars pass each other, searching the area.

From the corner of his eye, he noticed someone in one of the recessed entryways. He pulled out his cell phone and dialed 911. "This is Garrett Matthews, officer number 463, patch me through to the officers responding downtown to the shooting, immediately." He paused for a few seconds while the dispatcher put the call out.

"Go ahead, Officer."

"I'm off duty—in the apartment above the old bakery and can see someone hiding in the entry of the five-and-dime. He's moving…wait, it's one of the bartenders from the pub. Someone get him out of there."

He heard Amber yell to him from another room. "There's someone laying down in the alley."

"Just a minute, there's someone in the alley behind the bakery. Let me see what I can tell from here," he made his way toward her voice, trying to avoid crashing along the way. "Amber?"

"Back here. I think they've been shot."

TWELVE

Garrett saw Nick and a friend, Jeremy Logan, get out of their cars and an ambulance waiting around the corner until the police had secured the scene. After the gang task force had responded, Garrett went out and shared what little he could with them.

"What's going on between these gangs? Isn't this the third shooting this year?" Garrett directed the question to one of the gang task force officers.

He nodded. "Third shooting, and there's been one stabbing. That kid died. None of them are talking yet. They don't seem at all interested in making a deal for relocation, either."

"So besides gang affiliation, anything else behind their recent fighting?"

"The usual, wearing their colors, holding down turf, drawing the lines…" The officer lowered his head and shrugged. "I heard this guy mention TS— sometimes means 'Texas Syndicate,' a prison gang. We'll look into it."

"We have TS ties up here?"

"Thanks to the nation's prison system, we never know whose family problems and whose gang loyalties are going to show up on our doorsteps. I'm sure your brother can shed some light on the 'commerce' their families bring with them."

He nodded. "Let me know what you find out. And I'm not sure if everyone knows, but we do have a full-time resident living above the bakery. She's a friend of mine, so if you could…"

"We'll make note of that."

When he went inside, Amber was watching from her bedroom window, her arms wrapped around her. He stood in the doorway, concerned that crime had again, shattered her sense of security. "It's clear. Why don't we go downstairs and finish up the dishes so you can get some sleep."

She turned away from the window and walked toward him. "Is he, or she, alive?" she asked as she turned out the light and squeezed out the door, pulling him with her.

"Yes, he's alive. He was shot in the leg, looked pretty bad. Seems to be the latest ritual for gangs, maim but leave them alive. Amber," he said as he turned her toward him and looked him in the eye. "Are you okay?"

She rolled her head from side to side, then pulled her shoulders to her ears. "I think so. Could you stay here for a while longer…please?"

"Awhile. If you'd like, but we should really get back to my parents while there are officers around. I won't leave you alone, but I also don't want anyone to get the wrong impression. It's been okay at my folks, hasn't it?"

"Sure, but maybe all of this would stop if this creep knows you were here…" Her fear was apparent.

"I'm sorry, Garrett, I don't meant that. I'm a little shaky right now, but I need to get over this fear. I have to get used to staying alone. It's not the first time I've heard gunshots downtown."

"Do you call them in?"

She shook her head. "I haven't wanted to make enemies, since I'm here alone. And there aren't too many people living down here anymore, so if I call in, it's rather obvious."

"That's crazy."

"You're out there chasing down armed gangsters, Garrett, and you call me crazy? Someone has to be here in the middle of the night to get the baking done. After Nick and Sarah's warning, I knew it wasn't safe to come to work in the middle of the night. This is my solution. I need to be ready for the morning customers with fresh baked goods or I'm out of business. With City Hall and the courts still downtown, I might just survive until my wedding planning is bringing in the money."

He couldn't believe running her own business meant this much to her. "At least you have a comfortable place here so you don't have to come and go alone at night, but your phones going out are the third major incident this week." He looked around at the early twentieth-century architecture, amazed at how well they had been able to renovate it to keep up with all of her modern appliances. "And considering how old the building is, it's pretty well secured."

Amber nodded. "And we know that works. I'm relieved Papa had the security upgraded the year before he passed away. He was in and out of the hospital, and didn't want Nana here alone, but she wasn't about to give up her business to thugs. My parents pitched a fit, even then, but Papa installed the security system, and Nana ran it another ten years after that. I'll probably have to upgrade it as soon as business is stronger. The security company really wants me to do it now, but I can't afford it right now."

"The sooner the better." He had a feeling this was hitting her harder than she thought it would. He didn't want her to be alone here, but he also didn't feel it was appropriate to offer for the two of them to stay here alone. He had to convince her to find somewhere else to work from temporarily. He started in on the dishes, but Amber pulled him away.

"Wait a minute," she said, turning him around.

"Wait, yourself. I agreed to do the dishes. You can put them away." Though it had initially surprised him, Garrett liked the way Amber asserted herself and took business into her own hands.

"Oh, don't worry, I'm letting you do them." She pulled an apron from the shelf and wrapped it around him. "You'd better wear this. It gets pretty sloppy."

Garrett watched as she slipped the string over his head, then double-wrapped the apron strings around his waist and tied them. "Thanks, this is my good T-shirt, I'd hate to see it get dirty," he said sarcastically.

She just smiled. "If this cop thing doesn't work out, you look pretty good in an apron."

"I'll keep that in mind," he said, sticking his hands into the hot water and fishing around for a scouring pad. "I'm glad your grandfather was aware of what was happening around here. It's not been easy to see the changes in Old Town the last few years."

"Change is inevitable. God's plans couldn't come true if everything stayed the same. Without the adversity, would we ever feel the need to rely fully on God? I know until this week, I took that shield of refuge for granted."

Her wisdom was pretty frightening for someone so young. "I agree one hundred percent, but we can't ignore that sometimes that spiritual shield is also tested, and unfortunately, it's typically a high price to pay. I'd rather we didn't have to worry about gangs and guns, but I probably wouldn't have a job in that case. And yet, He called me into law enforcement, so I guess He'll provide a job somewhere for me." He rinsed another pan and set it in the steel draining rack. He wanted to make this one pile of dishes take forever, but he had to make sure Amber was able to get some sleep and still be safe for the night.

"I know you have a lot to do, but I'd feel better if you were doing this at Mom and Dad's…"

"Most nights I haven't worried, but after tonight I'll admit, I'm a little more nervous…. You probably will think it's naive, but I pray for safety every night when I drive up here alone. I pray for security for my business…." She took the large brownie pan, dried it and put it away. "I haven't had anything serious happen yet. Until the rock came in the window, that is."

"The police have been watching very closely in the area again, but that said, we had extra patrols in this area for months, and we can't be everywhere at the same time."

She shrugged. "I know. I'll be safe. I have a guardian angel watching over the place."

"Everyone needs one or two. Each of us boys carry a set of our grandfather's handcuffs on duty."

"Him, too? Wow, it really is in your blood, isn't it?"

"Pretty much," he said with a smile.

"That's so touching. Did he have a long career?"

Garrett nodded. "Thirty years," he said quickly, then deliberately changed the subject. "How'd you ever decide to go into business for yourself?"

Amber shook her head, a wistful look on her face. "I used to spend summers here with Nana and Papa. When I'd go home to Wyoming, I had all of these tasty recipes and ideas for parties. My friends started asking me for help planning their parties. I went to national cake decorating competitions, and wanted nothing more than to have my own shop. My parents refused to help me unless I got my college degree."

"You don't look old enough to have gone through college…where'd you go?"

Her cheeriness faded. "University of Wyoming, but I haven't finished. Not sure I will, actually. I'm too impatient to sit in a classroom for four years. What about you?"

"It wasn't easy sitting still, but I managed to make it through." He pushed her question aside, ignoring the details. He'd only been motivated to sit through seven years of college and two degrees to prove he could do it. "You're the oldest, aren't you?"

"Why?" She lifted her chin and rolled her blue eyes. "Just because I…"

"I didn't mean that in a negative way," he said, trying to make amends. "It's one of my hobbies, studying people, figuring out what makes them tick."

He also realized a relationship between an oldest and a youngest had about as bad odds of survival as police officer marriages. Then again, his family all had a long history of happily-ever-afters.

She pulled the huge pan from the rack and moved it to the top row of the baker's racks. "So you think people fit into stereotypes that easily, do you?"

He nodded. "Not perfectly, but there are common traits that are proven pretty accurate in most cases. Oldest children take charge. Good leaders..."

"So now I'm just a case, huh?" Amber smiled, elbowing him.

An hour later, they finished cleaning and Amber packed her wedding coordinating books to take along to his parents' house. He understood that smile, and the woman, now a lot more than he expected to ever understand any woman—despite the short time they'd known each other. He was beginning to wonder if he'd ever be able to leave her alone here at the end of an evening, even after this case was solved.

THIRTEEN

As Garrett and Amber closed up shop, she forgot something and ran back to get it. He went on to warm up his car. While he waited, he called his brother-in-law, the one married to his sister Kira. Hopefully, being an officer in a neighboring town wouldn't raise the kind of concerns that one of the FCPD digging would. "Dallas, I need a favor. Could you run a Nebraska plate for me?" He knew that he couldn't turn to anyone on the force to do his digging.

If someone was out to hurt the Matthews brothers, he wasn't going to give them any more rope to hang them with. Though the chief had told him to keep Amber out of the limelight, Garrett knew he would also be keeping a close eye on his every move. His cousin was keeping him informed about the investigation of the rock that had come through Amber's window. They were all trying to figure out what the note written on it meant, and who it was meant for.

He couldn't help but question why the chief wasn't pushing for an investigation if he suspected something was going on. Until Garrett had more to go on, he had to make his moves very carefully.

He scanned the street and unlocked his car, glancing up to Amber's apartment window, waiting for the lights to go on in her apartment.

"What's up, Garrett? Why don't you run it yourself?"

He and Dallas hadn't hit it off initially, but the whole family laughed about the incident now. After Kira's police ride-along had ended in a drug bust, with Kira the key witness, Dallas had gone to get a statement from Garrett's sister and ended up marrying her. "It's the case that led to my accident. I'm not sure I should be looking into it. In fact, I'm pretty sure I shouldn't be, but…"

"What in the world is going on over there? First Nick, now you? You don't think it could be someone with a grudge against you guys, do you?"

Garrett took a quick look under the car, kicking himself for letting himself assume anything—good or bad. He didn't watch cop shows on television for this reason. "No, I don't see how anyone could have carried this out to get at me. Amber, the woman who ran into me, didn't mean to hit me. She wouldn't hurt a flea."

Dallas chuckled. "Your sister and I are going to get to meet her, aren't we? Your parents sure seem to like her. They make it sound like you do, too."

He deserved the razzing. He'd dished it out, and now it was his turn to receive. "Just look up the information, Dallas." He paced the sidewalk and waited impatiently. Amber hadn't turned on the lights upstairs yet. He glanced around to the quiet block. There was no sign of gang problems now, but he really didn't like how long it was taking her to get her things.

If anyone could understand what Garrett was facing, dating a woman that he'd met in the line of duty, it was Dallas. "You still there?"

"I'm here."

"So while this is running, tell me more about this case," Dallas said.

Garrett could just imagine the smile on his brother-in-law's face as he explained the awkward situation with Amber and the superior officer who'd pushed him into her arms. "The last thing I want is to alert anyone at Fossil Creek P.D. that I'm digging into a closed case."

"And you still have no idea why they closed it?" Dallas asked.

Garrett was beginning to doubt the wisdom of enlisting his brother-in-law's assistance. He didn't expect Dallas to read him the riot act. "According to the chief, the mayor's put the gag order on it. Can't hurt business, you know."

"Despite the fact that innocent victims are paying the price…" Dallas finished.

Garrett heard his brother-in-law mutter under his breath. "Hey, the system just went down. I'll call you back when I find what you need."

Meanwhile, Garrett brushed his suspicions of corruption aside and got into the car. He called Nick to find out the status in the downtown area. They'd made several arrests within the rival gangs, but didn't think they had the shooter. The gang unit was having a busy night, and Garrett was sitting here, waiting for a light to go on. There was something wrong when he was more anxious to see a light in a second-story window than chasing down criminals.

It had been five minutes and Amber still wasn't upstairs. He pulled her business card from his wallet and dialed the shop number, since she'd sent her purse with him to the car. No one answered, though the phone sounded as if it was working again. He tried her cell number, hoping she'd put it into her pocket instead of her purse.

Just as he opened the car door to go inside, the lights in her apartment brightened the shades. "Don't open the shades, Amber," he whispered. Pretty soon her hand shone in the window and she waved. He smiled.

Amber finally came back out and locked the door behind her. She got into the car and shivered. "I don't know how, but I think the apartment is colder than when I went in ten minutes ago."

"Maybe you bumped into the thermostat."

"Maybe," she said, seeming worried.

"Were things okay? It seemed to take you a while."

She took a long time answering. "Yeah."

"Amber. What's wrong?"

She shrugged. "Probably nothing."

Garrett believed 100 percent in following his gut instinct, and right now he had a bad feeling. He looked into his rearview mirror, but didn't see anyone. "What's nothing?" He didn't want to scare her, but he did want to be prepared.

"I went to get my business credit card out of my desk upstairs and noticed that my knives weren't there where I put them after the accident."

"Why'd you put them in your desk?"

"I wasn't thinking straight. I just set them down there. But now they're not there. I kept meaning to move them back to the kitchen, but I've been so rushed. I'll need them for this weekend."

"You probably just put them away sometime and forgot. I'll help you look for them when we go back in the morning. I'm sure they're there somewhere."

Dallas called just as they pulled into his parents' driveway ten minutes later. He pulled a pad of paper from his glove box and a pen from the visor. "Hey, Dallas. What did you find out?"

"Marcus Smith, twenty-six years old, address on the registration is his parents' in Kearney, Nebraska, phone number 407-555-1212, no priors."

He wrote down the details and thanked Dallas. "We'll talk to you soon. Give Kira my love."

"Will do. Garrett, you're doing the right thing, but be careful that you don't cross the wrong person."

"When I figure out who that would be, I'll know who to watch out for, won't I? Thanks for the information."

As soon as they'd gone into the house, he reviewed Sam's notes and tried to figure a way to get more information about the original report to see if Chavez had filed any evidence at all

He checked his watch, realizing that Amber needed to be back at work in less than five hours. And he was going to be there to make sure she was okay.

Amber collapsed into bed, too tired to even think about all that had happened in the past four hours. The only thing left in her dreams was kissing the one man who should be off-limits—Garrett Matthews.

She woke at three in the morning, later than usual. She jumped out of bed, dressed and ran downstairs to meet Garrett. She'd have to shower and clean up as soon as Andrea and Sean showed up to work.

"Morning, beautiful."

"Hi, but I'm not beautiful right now. Sorry I'm late."

"With the two of us working, we'll be ready twice as fast. I think it's time I start learning the ropes."

The mixers were all running and the flour billowed from the bowls. She added a little more warm milk to the mixtures and all was back to normal, except the fine white dust all over the floor.

The shrill ring of the phone startled her and Garrett both. "Who would be calling at three in the morning?" She had to remember to attach a caller identification box to the business line. What if this was an emergency regarding Nana?

"At least the phone is working. I'll answer." All he got was heavy breathing.

"I've had a lot of hang-ups lately," Amber said. She couldn't believe she was so relieved that he was here. She pulled the dough from the mixers and covered them to rise. "I'm going to go upstairs to find my knives," she said. "Would you like to come up? I can make us breakfast."

He glanced at his watch and nodded. "I always work the night shift, so it's better for me to keep those hours while I'm off duty."

"You mean you didn't sleep last night?"

He shook his head. "I worked on the case mostly, but I hated to call the kid's parents so late."

Her smile disappeared. "I can't imagine making that call."

"It's a necessary part of the job, and it's going to be far easier than the next ones, I'm afraid. I'll call about six-thirty our time, in case they work. Hopefully about the time your employees arrive, I'll have some answers, then I can go home and rest for a while. So for now, what can I do to help you? Did you sleep?"

She stood there staring at him. "I was asleep before my head hit the pillow, but that's only because I feel so safe with you around."

Garrett smiled as he pulled her close. "Good."

"With your injury, you should be getting more sleep. And don't try to convince me you're better—you would have been released to work again."

His smile disarmed her. "I've been getting some alternative treatments so I won't have any medications in my system. I'm feeling fine," he insisted, placing a kiss on her forehead. "We're wasting time. Stop arguing and put me to work while I'm a willing slave." He passed by her and went right to the stairs to search her apartment for the missing knife set.

Amber unlocked the door, and the frigid air hit them in the face.

"Whoa, you weren't kidding. Is your furnace working?"

She paused. "It has been, but there's a draft." She walked back to the bedroom while he started looking for the thermostat.

Seconds later Amber's shrill scream set his adrenaline flowing. He heard a thud, and muffled screams.

He pulled his gun, pausing at each doorway ready

to take out whoever was threatening the woman he loved.

"Garrett," she squeaked.

Just as he got to the back room, he saw Amber drop to the floor and a dark figure run out the fire-escape door.

"Amber!" She didn't move.

He looked outside for the intruder, then slammed the door and dropped to her side. "Amber."

One of her huge chef's knives was on the ground next to her. "Amber," he said weakly, searching for a stab wound. He couldn't see that she'd been stabbed. He patted her face, then felt her carotid artery, ready to start CPR or whatever was necessary to save her.

Just as he adjusted her head, she gasped, then choked. "Garrett," she whispered. "He was here!"

"I know. Are you hurt?"

She shook her head. "I don't think so…" she said, softer this time. "It was him. It was the kidnapper."

He nodded. "He had a knife—are you sure he didn't…"

She sobbed, and Garrett pulled her into his embrace. "He…was in here…. The door was wide open, so I went to close it." She moved her hands to her throat. "He was behind the door when I went to close it. Said he'd been…waiting…for me." She pulled Garrett close. "And…" She stared at the knife on the floor next to them. "My knife? Was it *my* knife at my throat?"

"I don't know. It might have been. Don't touch it. Maybe he left prints." He needed to check her neck again. But how could he have missed a cut when he'd felt for her pulse?

She shook her head, pushing his hand from her neck. "No, he said you had everything, but no more. He said he's going to show you, outsmarting all of…all of you cops, and…"

Garrett was trying to make sense of her mumbling. "And what, Amber?" he whispered, his heart breaking for her. He caressed her back, trying to calm her down so he could understand her. He didn't ever want to let her go.

She looked at him with those crystal-blue eyes. He could drown in her eyes. If they ever had the chance, he could think of nothing he'd enjoy more.

She placed her hands on each side of his face. "He's going to kill…" She kissed him gently, then cried again.

He ran his fingers along her chin and noticed blood on his hand when he took it away. "Shh, you're okay now. He's gone. Amber, I need you to lie down and let me check your…" He could barely breathe, let alone speak. Surely he hadn't slit her throat. "I won't let that happen. We won't let him near you again, honey."

"No," she cried. "He's—"

"Amber, shh. Don't think about it. I'm going to call 911 now. I need to get my cell phone out of my pocket."

He let her loose, and she pulled him close and kissed him. "Don't leave me alone, Garrett. He's…going to kill you," she moaned. *"He's after you, Garrett."*

Garrett hoped his shock wasn't as apparent to her as it was to him. "I need to alert the police, Amber. And we have to get you checked out. Where's a clean shirt, or gauze, or…"

After making the call, he turned to her dresser and went for the largest drawer, hoping to find a cotton T-shirt to stop the bleeding. It was a shallow cut, but bleeding more than he dared let go.

She shook her head and stood. "I'm fine, aren't I?" she said so innocently he had to smile. She was going into shock.

He finally found a shirt, then picked her up and set her on the bed. "You look *very* fine. But I'm kind of biased. I'd like a medic to make sure." He forced a smile and looked at the cut. "It's not too bad," he lied, "but it's going to need a few stitches."

She passed out again. "I love you, Amber. I don't care if it's been a week or a decade, I'm always going to love you." He pressed his lips to her forehead and said a prayer. "Heavenly Father, I know You aren't so cruel to bring my bride to me and take her away so soon." He felt tears sting his eyes. He pressed her cotton shirt to her throat, vowing silently to find this thug.

Ten minutes later the chief stormed into her apartment bellowing orders to get fingerprints and scour the scene for evidence. Finally he wanted answers.

He'd called his parents, who went to the hospital to watch out for Amber while he met with the detectives, going through everyone he could have ticked off in his short career. For the next three hours Garrett was again on the other side of the badge, and he didn't like it. He needed answers. He needed to figure out who could hate him enough to kill him, and anyone in the way.

By noon, Amber had been released with fifteen stitches. She'd gone home with his mother, and he and his father had come to her place to board up the window, find the essentials for her to work on the wedding cake at his parents' house, and throw out the blobs of dough, which had risen all over the proofing oven.

Until this guy was caught, he had to convince her to officially close her business. Sarah and Nick had gone to watch the house. He wasn't taking any more chances assuming anywhere was safe. This guy had picked his way into a steel fire door. This time he'd bypassed the shop and went right to her home.

The crime scene had been picked clean, and crime tape was across all the doors into her apartment. Black fingerprinting dust covered everything.

Still, there was no time to waste, for any of them.

Three hours later, while Amber rested, Garrett made the phone call to find out how he could get hold of the owner of the yellow SUV. He made the call, then hurried out the door.

Amber greeted Andrea and Sean, then excused herself to shower and get ready for her final appointment with the bride of the week. "If Maya Brewer arrives early, have her take a seat. I'll be right down."

She'd just finished her shower and putting her makeup on when Grace Matthews called upstairs to tell her that the bride-to-be was here and in a panic over Amber's emergencies.

Maya hugged Amber when she heard what had happened. "I heard there's another storm expected this weekend. Are you *sure* that you won't have a problem getting the cake up to the resort?" Maya asked without taking a breath as Amber tried to remain patient.

"I have it under control," she said confidently, even if she was a nervous wreck just thinking about it. It had only been twelve hours since the attack. She wanted to give Maya a guarantee, but her life had no more guarantees.

She pulled out her notebook and reviewed all the times and details with the bride. "I'm scheduled to arrive at noon Friday with the cake and the mints. The flowers will be delivered that afternoon. I confirmed the menu for three hundred."

"Three hundred? I thought we told you four, to be safe." Customers like Maya were the reason Amber wrote every detail into the agreement. By the date of the event, there were always questions.

Amber pulled up the scanned document of their final contract. "We settled on three hundred. The other one hundred was going to cost you a bundle," she gently reminded Maya. "The hotel prepares for an extra ten percent, so you have enough food for 330 guests. How many more RSVPs did you receive this week?"

"Twenty-four."

Amber included that on her documentation and added it up. "That's 305 guests with eight days to go. I think you're fine. It's not uncommon for a few cancellations to come at the last minute to offset those who forget to return their responses."

She went through her list of final reminders, printed them out and gave the bride a copy. As they went through them, Amber highlighted those that the bride needed to do between now and the wedding. It was a good reminder for Amber, as well.

When Maya left an hour later, exhaustion from the past few days set in.

That night, Garrett and Amber sat in front of the fire in his parents' family room, counting their blessing for being alive.

"Who do you think it was, Garrett?"

"I don't know." He held her in the crook of his arm, brushing her hair off her forehead. "We don't have to talk about that, Amber." But he couldn't stop thinking about it, either. He couldn't stop wondering who could hate him that much.

"What else is there to talk about?" Amber said. "That the police have cut off my livelihood, or that a murderer has me afraid to go home or run my business?"

"It's for your own safety."

She gazed into his eyes. "Will it ever be safe again? Not just for me, but my customers, too?"

"We'll sure do what we can to help you get business booming again. For now, Mom and Dad offered to lend you their van to get everything to the resort."

"Your dad told me, and I wish I knew a way to thank them, but I really couldn't under these circumstances." She looked into Garrett's eyes, wondering if the intensity of her feelings for Garrett would ever fade. "Would you come with me?"

"There's only one person who would keep me away. And if it means staying here in Fossil Creek in order to keep you safe, that's what I'll do. If I can't go, Dad would probably drive you if you'd feel better."

Tears silently fell, and she moved to rest her head on his firm shoulder. "I can't believe how close we came…."

Garrett noticed his high school yearbooks on the bookshelf and wondered if there was someone from high school he'd made mad enough to hold a grudge. Someone he'd seen with handcuffs. He jumped from his seat, surprising Amber.

"What's wrong?"

He pulled four books from the shelf. "I've been trying to think where I've seen someone with handcuffs. In high school I was in the Explorers, a club of kids interested in law-enforcement careers. No one was very good with handcuffs, and since we didn't ever really cuff anyone, there wasn't too much emphasis on their use. Maybe that was where I saw that interesting technique. I can't even get a definite time line. I kept trying to place him in my police academy classes. Not only does that not make any sense, it's terrifying to consider."

Amber took one of the yearbooks and looked at the front. "A decade is a long time to hold a grudge. I can't believe you've made anyone *that* mad, Garrett. He wants you…dead. He said he wants to hurt you."

"The rock…it wasn't meant for you. And it wasn't gang related. It was a message to me. He must have seen me there earlier that night. Why the tires?" He thumbed to the index and looked for Explorers under clubs, then turned to the page it was featured on. He read through the list of names, Amber looking over his shoulder. "Anyone look familiar?"

"Uh-uh," she mumbled as she studied the photo. "These were kids who were interested in being police officers? Wouldn't they have to be pretty clean-cut kids?"

Garrett was busy reading, and didn't hear all of what she'd said. "What?"

She repeated her questions. "So what in the world could you have done that would make one of them want to hurt you and people you care about?"

He thought for a while. "A lot of them were straight-A students, but there were a couple who had tough family lives. Alcoholic parents, abuse…there was one kid I inadvertently got kicked out of the group. He was hanging around with some gang members at one of my football games. When I got home from the game, I asked my dad about the rules…and the guys I'd seen him with. He never came back." Garrett quickly scanned the photo. "He's not in this one. Look in the others. I don't remember which year he joined."

She looked, but didn't see anyone in the club photos who looked at all familiar. "Do you remember his name?"

"Anthony something…" Garrett paced the room while Amber looked up every Anthony listed. "Anthony," he whispered over and over.

"Maybe Dad would remember—just a minute." He took off for the stairs.

"Garrett, he's probably asleep. It can wait until morning, can't it?"

"Well, I guess so. Depends on who is next on his list, though. He wants to torture me. Dad never forgets names, especially of the thugs."

The next day Amber had a surprise delivery when she and Garrett stopped at the shop to meet the installation men from the security and glass companies. The sign company dropped off the magnetic signs for the cars, and wanted to start on the storefront sign that afternoon. She held up a colorful automobile sign. She baked several batches of rolls for one of her best customers and had the boxes with her. "May as well have CiCi try them out this morning, see if it helps avoid parking tickets."

After the attack Amber was apprehensive of making additional investments. "They're seriously going to do the storefront today?" Amber had been so excited about it a week ago. "Finally it will officially be my store—Parties Galore and now I'm too scared even to try to make a go of it again."

"Don't let this creep steal your dreams, Amber. We'll get through this," Garrett insisted. "God didn't bring you this far for you to give up. No matter what you do, you'll have struggles, but God is always there to get you through."

Sean had shown up to help. "If you haven't thought of it already, we should call the paper to do a ribbon-cutting ceremony."

Garrett agreed. "But you should wait until we catch this guy."

Amber smiled at the thought. "Sean, that's a brilliant idea. Let's figure out how quickly we can pull this together. I don't want to give that creep a chance to gloat—not another day! I'm thinking we should either do it on the weekend after this huge wedding, or at least that next Monday, so I can bake extra to have free samples. Hey, the parade of the holiday lights is coming up soon. Maybe we should plan to have the grand opening that weekend. We could piggyback on their advertising."

Her mind was moving a mile a minute with possibilities and, after hearing Amber's excitement to keep her business going, Garrett offered his full support.

"Sean, the city council's requirements are on the city's home page. Contact the mayor's office and…"

"It's right up my alley. Leave it all to me."

She read his mind and smiled. "It's going to be one of your business-planning projects, isn't it?"

Sean nodded. "Okay, so it wasn't an original idea…"

With a laugh, Amber shook her head. "You can test all of your ideas on my business, Sean. Just don't make me go through the class with you. Deal?"

Amber called the sign company and confirmed the installation for after lunch. She hung up and squealed, giving Garrett a hug. "It's really going to be okay again, isn't it?"

"It will be bigger and better than ever," Garrett said.

FOURTEEN

After the front window was installed, the men from the security company got started, and Garrett went to a meeting he'd scheduled with the chief. Nick and Sarah both came to stand guard in his absence. Amber and Sarah had fun talking about their New Year's Eve surprise wedding party. They were having a private ceremony and a party for friends and family to bring the New Year in together.

"Let me see your stitches," Sarah said, and Amber lifted her head, feeling the tug on the wound.

"Did they do a good job on them?" Amber asked. "I can't see them without reflecting them into two mirrors, and they still looked jagged."

Sarah studied them again. "They look smooth from here. How're you doing?"

Amber shrugged. "Some minutes I feel really brave and like I'm fine, and then an instant later I'm crying at how close it was."

"That's good. Normal, I mean. Don't be hesitant to talk to someone if it doesn't start getting less and less often that you're feeling that way."

"Is it also normal that I was mad that Garrett stayed with me and didn't go after him?"

"You don't want the guy to hurt anyone else. That's pretty understandable."

"But now…I'm scared for Garrett's safety every time he's out of my sight. I don't know how you deal with the danger every day—for you, and for Nick."

Sarah smiled. "We make the most of the time we have together. I know he won't take foolish chances, and I think he believes that I won't, either. I hope so, anyway. It's a lot different when you have someone waiting for you at the end of the day. I was a lot more willing to put myself on the line and take stupid chances when I was truly single. Not that the rest of my family and friends didn't matter, but…it's just a lot nicer having Nick."

Amber laughed. "Falling in love is overwhelming to the senses."

"This from a wedding planner? Now, that's frightening," Sarah exclaimed.

Amber blushed. "I think that's why it's overwhelming. I had the image of the perfect 'look' of love and romance. And when it happened to me, I didn't think it was real." The smile disappeared. "Not until I realized how quickly I could lose Garrett. Funny thing is one crime introduced us, and a different one threatens to tear us apart."

"Once we know for sure who we're looking for, he doesn't stand a chance of getting away again."

"I hope he's caught soon."

The fire-escape door had to be replaced, and Amber ordered the top of the line for security. No matter whether it would be her living here or anyone else, she didn't want a repeat of this incident. The windows, while old and not very well insulated, were almost impossible for an adult to break in to or climb into from outside. Being on the second floor, she'd had a false sense of security that could never be replaced.

Garrett had taken his yearbooks into the precinct, hoping that it would give them some clues.

Now Garrett was back, and he didn't look happy.

"What's wrong, Garrett?"

He glanced at her, then at her staff. "We have a missing person report filed. She fits the description you gave."

Amber's relief at his safe return fell through to the cellar. "Who is she?"

"Could we talk somewhere privately?" he said, sounding very official. And very police officer-like.

She didn't like the tone in his deep voice.

Amber looked at Andrea and Sean, pausing to collect her thoughts. "We'll be upstairs if you need us...I mean, if you need me."

She glanced at Garrett, wondering why this was so hush-hush. Surely he realized she'd shared this information with her employees after all that had happened. She flipped the light switch on and hurried up the stairs, anxious to know more.

After the door closed behind them, she turned to face him. "So what did you find out? Is she okay?"

"Her name is Jenna Miller—five-eight, slim build, auburn hair..."

She closed her eyes, seeing the girl all over again. She nodded.

"She totaled her compact car in the last snowstorm.

Her boyfriend is going to University of Nebraska at Lincoln and lives on campus, so he let her borrow his SUV until Christmas break. He hasn't heard from her since that afternoon…they were on the phone when she saw the police officer walking up to her window. Jenna asked Steve, the boyfriend, if his plates were expired."

Amber closed her eyes and felt the tears well at her eyes. "Were they?"

He shook his head. "No, but she told him she'd call him back after she got things straightened out. He's been trying to reach her, but she isn't answering her cell phone. He got hold of her roommate. She insisted Jenna had been in and out, that their paths had just crossed. Her boyfriend is on his way here. I've called her parents in Alaska, talked to her roommate and asked Nick to look up a few theories of mine."

"No one suspected anything was wrong?"

He shrugged. "Campus police didn't know about our case, because it wasn't…" Garrett paced the room. "What's done is done. We need to go on from here. The parents filed a report with campus police. It's faster for them to get into her school records than if city government got involved right now."

"But it didn't happen on campus…"

"Technically, no, but since she's a missing student, our first priority is finding her. They can move faster on most issues with campus policy being slightly more forgiving than the city and state governments would be."

She opened her eyes and admired Garrett, appreciating his sensitivity and determination to keep digging into this, even though he shouldn't be.

"Once they verify that the last day she was in class was Thursday, they'll pull Fossil Creek Police Department in, and the chief will have no more excuses not to open a full investigation."

"Have you told him yet?"

He shook his head. "Campus police are going to call me when they're ready to issue a warrant. I'll happen into the chief's office…to talk to him about getting back to work. I'm not supposed to be investigating this, Amber."

"Then why are you? Haven't I already caused you enough trouble?"

He shrugged.

"Something tells me you shouldn't be here, legally, I mean, and…and now I'm to blame for you disobeying your boss's orders, too."

Garrett shook his head. "You didn't make me do this. It's the right thing to do."

"Then why didn't the lieutenant investigate in the first place? Why didn't Samantha Taylor do it? Nick knew about it. Sarah knew about it. Why you, Garrett? It seems to me that if it wasn't for me, you wouldn't be doing this, would you?"

He didn't answer right away.

Was that a good sign? Or was he regretting getting involved in the first place? "I was more driven to push this because I believe you, yes. But I was never doing it simply to win you over, if that's what you're concerned about." The corner of his lips twitched. "If you hadn't run into me and I wasn't on mandatory leave, no, I wouldn't be doing this off the radar. I'd have been the first man in line after that creep. So don't even think of blaming yourself." He tried to pull her close again, but she shook her head. "You mentioned at the accident that you'd pray for me, right?"

She held her head high. "Yes."

"I appreciate it. I want you to understand my relationship with God, Amber. I'm a Christian first, a Christian man second, and a Christian officer third. My first obligation is to God, to do what He commands. And that would never allow me to use you—period. Second, I need to be true to myself—I'm still trying to figure out exactly what God has planned for me, as a Christian man. Is that career, or marriage? I thought it was one, and now I'm thinking He has the other in mind. And third, I believe God led me to law enforcement to uphold the laws that man has created for our society. I *am* a cop, and I can't turn that off, so one way or another, I would be digging into this case, no matter whether you're involved or not. As a Christian man, I really want to believe God had a reason for bringing us together."

"I hope so, Garrett." The butterflies in her stomach were back. All these years she'd seen only one side of police officers. She wanted to believe that Garrett was different than those officers, but her heart was still skeptical. She wanted Garrett to be right, to believe that God had a reason for their accident. She didn't believe their attraction was simply that—attraction. She felt too much for it to be just that, but it was too far-fetched to believe it was serious already. Believing it was true meant letting herself care for Garrett, and that made him that much more dangerous.

He said it himself, he'd always be a cop. If nothing

else, she owed him the truth about her past. Her wild years. Her lack of trust in police officers.

"I need to work through how I'm going to tell the chief about this, but we're still on for dinner tonight, right?"

She nodded silently.

"Should we make it early, about six?"

"That would be fine," she said, mentally calculating how long she could ignore that she was totally wrong for Garrett. She had already hurt him, she couldn't make matters worse. Because as soon as he found out she had a police record, it would be over.

FIFTEEN

Garrett had a long day ahead. After questioning Amber again, she realized both the suspects fit the same description. They'd gone back through his yearbook and finally found him. He'd done as much as he could to find a current address for Anthony Melendez without access to police records. There was nothing. How could he vanish? Now it was time to have patience—something God hadn't given him enough of, apparently, because He kept testing Garrett on it.

He wanted to head over to the precinct and wait for the university police, but knew better than to push the chief. He'd been doing the stretching exercises that the physical therapist had suggested and felt like he could get back to the streets any day now.

He tried to rest, but that was futile and he knew it. He couldn't seem to get this case, or Amber Scott, off his mind. He accessed his work e-mail from home, but there wasn't much to get excited about there, either. Garrett jotted notes about Amber's description of the incident into his notepad adding in possible evidence from Samantha Taylor's notes and from the break-in at the store. He needed to be ready to push the investigation as soon as he got the word. His mind came back to the suspect. He'd gotten his aunt to e-mail him a copy of the sketch she'd done from Amber's description to connect it to Melendez's current mug shot.

Tapping the arm of the worn-down sofa, Garrett closed his eyes and walked back through time. He remembered that goofy maneuver with the handcuffs. He wondered how long it would've taken him to make the connection to Melendez had he not happened to notice his yearbooks on the shelf. He hadn't wanted to consider that they could've been dealing with a rogue officer who was on active duty.

Not that it was out of the question, since two crooked cops had tried to implicate his brother in their drug ring. Maybe Melendez had applied to the academy or to FCPD. If Garrett's report to his dad had kept Melendez from his dreams—why had he gone to the other extreme to discredit FCPD? Or maybe this was just another attempt to frame the Matthews brothers.

It wasn't long until Chief Thomas, himself, called him into the station. A half hour later, he had showered, shaved and was waiting, in uniform, hoping beyond all hopes that this would all come together quickly so they could get back to work.

The chief's secretary, Phyllis, led Garrett right into his office. "Afternoon, Garrett."

Garrett nodded. He wasn't in the mood to make small talk. He filled the chief in on what he and Amber had found. The chief called the investigator to start looking for the suspect.

"University police have a report of a missing girl. They're getting ready to make an announcement, but with the attack on Amber Scott possibly connected, we'd better talk to them ASAP. For the record, Garrett, the mayor isn't happy, but he did admit that he was wrong."

"What can I do?"

"If you can get the doctor to clear you, we could use your help with surveillance in the downtown area to catch Melendez. After the shooting the other night, business owners were concerned, but after what Melendez did to Amber, there's an uprising. Ms. Scott isn't the only business owner ready to go to newspapers."

Garrett felt his lip twitch, threatening to share his personal opinion about the situation. "I'm scheduled to go for a check-up tomorrow afternoon."

"That will do. Will you be working at the bakery tonight?"

"No, she's working from my parents' house to fill the orders she had, but until the security's set up and she's sure it's safe for customers to go back, there's no walk-in business. I don't think she'd have a problem with me working there for a few more days, if that's what you're asking," he said, cautiously avoiding answering the chief's question directly. *Lord, help me to handle this professionally, yet without upsetting Amber, either.*

The chief glanced at the same file that he'd studied the last time they'd visited. "Have you found anything else out about the incident she witnessed?"

"Just that the suspect didn't know how to use handcuffs. But the odd thing is, I was sure I'd seen someone, somewhere hold them like she described." He demonstrated with his grandfather's cuffs. "I kept coming up empty on where I might have seen it, until last night. I realized a kid named Melendez and I were in the Explorers at the same time, until I saw him with some of the more prominent gang-bangers. I asked Dad about it, he was never there again. So if he wanted to be a cop, I can see him buying a uniform to get revenge."

"It's so easy to buy them off the Internet now, I would have been surprised if he had picked one up locally. Detective Wang has been contacting online stores, looking for orders from this region. There's been nothing in the time period of our reports, so either he lived outside this region when he ordered it, or he bought it in a store with cash, or secondhand."

Garrett couldn't help but consider the kind of person that would do this, and Anthony fit. He'd wanted to fit in somewhere. "Is there a pattern with the victims? I don't understand how he picked these victims. Is anyone looking at that?"

The chief smiled. "Haven't found one yet. Would you care to give it a shot?" He slid the file across the desk. "He's getting more careless, and more brazen, that I can tell you."

He stared at the file, still cautious of the way all of this was playing out. The detectives had far more experience than he did with investigations. He wasn't sure he had any of the right theories, either.

"Kidnapping a young woman before dark right off campus definitely wasn't smart." He read the first page of the report, dated three months ago. Nine forty-five on a Sunday evening. A high school student had been a block from home when she'd seen the police lights. She'd been too frightened to stop, and called her parents for advice. They'd advised her to calmly drive the rest of the way home and they met her outside. When she pulled to a stop in front of their house, the unmarked car drove on past the house. Though they had called the police, the suspect had disappeared before anyone from patrol had been able to make it to the area.

No description of the suspect.

Garrett looked at the address, hoping it would give them the break they needed. Flipping through the pages beneath, he found a city map where they had already started mapping the different reported incidences.

The second incident was roughly three weeks later, in the college area and involved a twenty-two-year-old student who had no cell phone when the police car, also white with a bubble light, pulled her over. The victim had become nervous when he approached the window and ordered her to get out of the vehicle. When she refused, he broke her window out with a flashlight. She had cuts and bruises from the glass and the flashlight hitting her, but she was able to put the car in gear and get away. Caucasian or Hispanic male, mustache, roughly twenty years old. Police uniform, gun, flashlight.

"Where are the suspect sketches?"

"The first victim never saw the guy. Second one couldn't give us a good enough description for Meg to release it, you've probably seen Amber's suspect...."

The third victim hadn't reported it until the next morning, when her roommate took her to the emergency room for stitches. Though she hadn't admitted to as much, likely reason she hadn't reported it was that she'd been driving while under the influence. She'd been at a party until somewhere around midnight.

Time wasn't consistent. Description similar to Amber's, if one didn't consider race, or facial hair.

She wasn't sure exactly of her location, and due to the call not coming in immediately, there had been no investigation.

He looked up at the chief and shook his head. "We should have issued a public warning long ago."

"Even if it had gone out, there's no assurance that it would have stopped any of the reported incidences. Personal safety and police stops are discussed in all of our community safety courses."

The fourth incident he knew far too much about, but he read the case report to see what Lieutenant Chavez had included. To his surprise, all of the information that Samantha had given him was included. So who had dropped the ball? Why had no one followed up with Amber?

There was another report of an incident that took place last night, on the north side of campus, just two blocks from Old Town. The victim had called 911 and had been advised to drive to the nearest grocery store parking lot and a marked car would meet her there. She couldn't give any information about the suspect. Something had apparently spooked him. He'd evaded the police again.

"So we have a missing student, but there's still no sign of the victim from last week?"

The chief shook his head. "At least we have a probable identity now." He confirmed that the information he'd found matched the official report from the university police. Garrett listened, waiting for the chief to let on that he had contacted the family. If Thomas knew, he didn't let on.

"When were they last in touch with her?"

"The boyfriend was on the phone with her when the suspect made contact with her. He's taking it hard."

"Yeah," he said, not wanting it to be obvious that he already knew all of this.

"Her parents have been trying to get in touch with her for almost a week. She last left them a message the day before the boyfriend talked to her. Her parents pushed her to transfer here, to save money on tuition," the chief added. "Imagine how much guilt they're feeling right now. I don't like the direction this is heading."

Garrett liked it even less. If Amber was now a witness to a crime linked to the Texas Syndicate, that meant she, too, could have a shadow for the rest of her life. "I want twenty-four-hour protection ordered for Amber until we figure out who Melendez's accomplices are."

The chief agreed. "Done, but under my conditions. I'm not going to try to provide protection for the entire staff and customers. If she wants to stay safe, she's going to have to keep the shop closed down until we have more information to go on."

Garrett didn't say anything. He couldn't. He

couldn't do this to Amber. He had to find another option. How could he convince her he had fallen in love with her at the same time he took her dream away? Garrett closed his eyes and prayed fervently for God's wisdom. The only scripture that came to mind was from the Book of Samuel, a prophet who, through his own trials and triumphs, was rewarded with God's blessing. *The promise of the Lord proves true; He is a shield for all those who take refuge in Him. Shield Amber from harm, Father, and let us both find a life of refuge with You.*

Garrett could hear Chief Thomas moving papers, and opened his eyes.

"Somehow, I didn't think you'd like those conditions, but I think once you get past your personal feelings, you'll understand."

"I don't understand. And she'll go for them even less."

The chief pushed a manila envelope across the desk. "You don't have to read it now, but I think it might be of interest. You can keep it."

Garrett turned the envelope over and noticed it was sealed. He tried to focus on the impersonator case, but everything had changed.

He'd fallen in love. And he would do everything within his power to protect the woman that God had brought into his life.

"Last night's victim," Garrett managed to say, "How old was she and what time did the incident happen?"

They discussed more facts and more theories for another hour, until Garrett could hardly stand the thought of Amber in her shop, any time of day with anyone. After they finished, Garrett changed into his street clothes, keeping his bulletproof vest on. He placed his weapon and an additional couple of magazines of ammunition in his duty bag. If he was going to be coming and going at all hours downtown, he was going to be prepared.

SIXTEEN

Amber left a message for Garrett two hours ago. Now that security had been fixed, she hated to take this mess to his parents' house. She was far too behind and far too tired to let herself be distracted. She only had a few more to finish after Nick and Sarah had needed to leave.

She needed to talk to God about what He had in mind, throwing her and Garrett together. Now, of all times, when he was applying for special-agent jobs, and she was working sixteen hours a day trying to build her business. She'd prayed for Garrett's recovery, about her feelings for Garrett and now it was time to pray that she could let him go before they got too involved. They had to be realistic.

Heavenly Father, I beg You to take this confusion away. I don't know how I can love Garrett so soon. Sweet, loveable, protective men like him don't go for girls like me. He's a take-the-bull-by-the-horns kind of guy, and I'm a bossy oldest child who has trouble taking orders. Or accepting advice. Even from those who mean well. "I don't care about an uptown shop with a fancy showroom," she said softly. "I'm happy here in Nana's shop, God. I don't want to have a security service watching my doors, seeing who is coming and going, but right now, I'm very thankful to have them."

She filled her cake-decorating bag with pink royal icing, then moved to the sofa with a tray in front of her. The pastel hibiscus were flowers made from royal icing and would take a day or two to dry, and time was getting short. After loosely forming the foil square to the flower nail, she spun the nail into position between her thumb and her forefinger. She squeezed the bag and moved the rose tip up and down the bowl of the nail, quivering slightly to give the edge the ruffled look of a natural flower. She added the candied stamens and set it on the cookie sheet to dry.

Her mind returned again and again to Garrett, and how to tell him about her past. How to tell him it was over between them. Or more to the point, how to prepare herself for that reality. She went back and forth, just like the repetitive motions of making flowers for the wedding cake. A pastel wedding in the mountains, right before Thanksgiving.

She shook her head, wishing she hadn't sent Nick and Sarah away until she'd heard from Garrett. She was getting worried that he hadn't called back. She hoped Melendez hadn't found him this time.

It was for the best, she kept telling herself. They'd been attracted to each other since their vehicles had collided. This couldn't be anything more than a reaction to the stress, guilt and physical attraction. They had to put some distance between them, she tried to convince herself.

The business phone rang, and Amber heaved a sigh of relief. The last thing she felt like doing tonight was going out and trying to enjoy herself. She had too many details to finish for this big wedding, she reminded herself as she picked up the phone.

She knew he'd call, and she was ready to argue that she was fine. Unfortunately, it was Rachelle, and her best friend wasn't in the mood to be put off. After talking about the kids, her husband, and the added stress of the holidays, she asked, "Have you heard the public announcement?"

"Yeah, I did," she said hesitantly. With their vacation, Amber hadn't wanted to worry them with her crises.

"I'm wondering what happened to make them decide to release the information," Rachelle said.

Amber moved the speaker phone closer so she could work and talk. "Garrett insisted the mayor didn't want them to make it public, so Garrett did a little digging and made contact with her family." Then Amber told Rachelle what had happened to her.

"Are you okay with him being a cop? He seems like a nice guy," she said, expressing her concern with Amber for staying at the store alone.

Amber assured her it was safe again, and the police were watching out for her, thanks to Garrett.

Amber bit her lip and the happiness spread, just hearing that her friend liked what she'd heard about Garrett. "He is a really nice guy, but I know he's trying to get a job with the FBI or one of those federal agencies. The last thing he needs is someone holding him back. He's a good officer, but I don't think I'd be able to take the stress."

"Don't give up without talking to Garrett, Amber. Hand it to God and give it a chance. Maybe you can get him to come to church Sunday. If you really care for him, you need to compromise. God will take care of the rest. I'd like to meet him," Rachelle said.

Amber could hear the smile in her friend's voice. "This is just because of the case," she said, trying to prepare herself for that fact. Sure, he'd been comforting after the attack, but sooner or later, it would come down to facing reality. He had dreams that didn't go along with hers.

They talked for a long time while she worked on the flowers for the cake.

"I guess we'll see, but he seems pretty serious. I mean, you're practically part of his family now!"

"They are as easy to love as he is, honestly."

Rachelle laughed. "See? You need to give it a chance!"

Amber explained that she needed to tell Garrett about her police record, before things got any more involved. It helped to say the words aloud, to hear her friend finally support her reasoning.

An hour later, she'd covered every pan she had in the family-size kitchen with pastel flowers and set them on every available table and seat to dry, and she still had another color left to make. Amber thanked Rachelle for making a long, quiet afternoon go quicker. They said goodbye, and Amber again wondered what was keeping Garrett.

It was only five o'clock. She may as well make the last color of royal icing and know they were all ready. Dumping powdered sugar, dried egg whites and water into the home-size professional mixer, she cranked it up, then left it to whip for ten minutes. She took a deep breath and felt the stitches on her jaw, reminding her that God did answer her prayers.

She turned on the radio and, almost immediately, the public announcement came on. The police advised women to be extra cautious and on the lookout for a police impersonator. They included a description of the car and the man. They even went so far as to advise anyone who was suspicious of being stopped by an unmarked car in a dark secluded area to call 911 from their cellular phone or, if they didn't have a phone, to cautiously drive to a busy location before stopping. If it was a legitimate officer, they would be patient and support that action. It all sent chills up Amber's spine. *Trust God. Let Him handle it.*

She switched to a radio station that played praise music and went to look out the window. A light snow was falling. She noticed an SUV like his parents' drive past and felt the loneliness sink in again.

"That's ridiculous," she whispered. "It couldn't be Garrett. He had to have gotten my message. He would have called by now." She twisted the shade closed again and tried to focus on the music as she got ready to sit and finish the last batch of flowers. She moved some of the trays to the bed so she'd have room to bring another tray up from the shop. She hurried down the stairs, into the bakery kitchen and grabbed one of the giant cake pans to store the next batch in.

The phone rang again, and she didn't want to get her hopes up again. She stared at the phone with fear, remembering the heavy breather who had called her before the attack. "Parties…"

"It's Garrett," he interrupted.

"Hi," she said, relieved. The feeling of warmth spread. "Is that you that I saw drive by?"

He laughed. "I wasn't sure if you were still here. Nick has been watching out as he patrols. I waited to call until I saw lights. I know you said you want some space, but there's something I need to talk to you about. I'm out front, if you have a few minutes."

"Yeah, we do need to talk. I'm in the kitchen, so I'll be right there to let you in." She set the receiver on the hook and grabbed the key from under the counter.

She disarmed the new security system, then opened the door and hurried him inside. "I've got royal icing mixing upstairs. It should be ready. Come on up after you've locked the door. The alarm will go back on automatically in sixty seconds. You know where the coat hook is and where the key goes, right?"

"Yep," he said as he took off his coat and shook the snowflakes from the parka. She turned and ran up to her apartment.

He turned the key to lock the deadbolt and watched her disappear with a cake pan in her hands. "And I suspect I'm going to learn where you keep a lot more of your supplies before long," he said, to himself, he realized. She was long gone.

He hung the key on the hook under the counter and walked through the immaculate kitchen, appreciating how much effort it had taken to get it that way.

He turned the corner to head up the stairs, a sweet aroma smacked him in the face.

Sugar. How could it smell any sweeter than a bakery did every day?

Nothing could have prepared him for seeing her apartment with trays of pink and lavender and yellow and soft blue candy flowers all over. "What happened in here?" He looked around the room again. "It looks like Easter eggs exploded all over."

She looked at the mess and smiled wryly. "Flowers for the wedding cake this weekend."

"You actually make them?" There was barely room to walk. "I guess I assumed bakeries bought them from a flower supplier or someone."

Amber bit her lip, struggling to hold on to the happiness. "You can buy them, but I am a professional cake decorator," she said.

"Interesting choice for a November wedding, isn't it? That is, according to Sarah and my sister. It seems like I just keep hearing discussions of weddings these days."

She laughed. "I agree with them, but I couldn't change Maya's mind. They didn't decide to get married until a couple of months ago, and didn't want to wait until spring. But Easter is her favorite holiday."

Garrett chuckled.

"I hope it works, or I'm going to be storing a lot of flowers. At least they store well, so I can have them on hand for summer weddings."

"Now I know why my mom always bought our cakes here. The flowers look so real." No matter how light the conversation, Garrett could feel the tension between them. He blamed himself for moving so quickly, before their friendship had fully developed.

He stuffed his hands in his pockets and stared at her. He couldn't stall anymore. "We need to talk, Amber."

For a long moment Amber looked back at him, then returned the decorating bag to the counter and covered it with a wet cloth. "Yes. We do," she said, leaning one hip against the counter. "I wondered why it took you so long to call back."

He nodded. "The chief and I had a lot to discuss. That, and a few other things. He gave me an unexpected file to read. Yours."

Her smile faded, a slow, painful evaporation of sweet beauty. "If you don't mind, I need to keep working, this frosting dries rock hard, and…"

"What can I do to help?"

She stared awkwardly at him, frozen in place. "You're staying?"

"Unless you want me to leave. I just got here, but if you don't want to talk…" He stared back, determined to keep his distance. Nothing was going to be accomplished if they couldn't talk through difficult issues like these. He held his breath, worried that she was going to send him away.

She grabbed her supplies, walked over to the sofa and started working away. "Actually, it's rather frightening the way God works. I was just wondering how to ask if you had seen my police record…."

"I hadn't, until my meeting with the chief today."

She paused, the frosting heaping into a blob on the spindle in her hand. "I'm sorry, I shouldn't have assumed that you'd check me out first…."

He shrugged. "I wouldn't be the first officer to fall for a bad girl." He smiled, noting that she didn't laugh at his humor. "I'm joking."

"I warned you that I wasn't the girl of your dreams," she said, going about her business. "But then again, your major objective was to keep me out of the way, wasn't it?"

"What's that supposed to mean?"

Amber acted like she didn't hear—which he might have considered if she wasn't breathing faster than normal. She poked the foil squares into several cups of the nail-looking things and eased the flaps over the edge, then filled each with frosting petals and carefully pulled them off the nail and set them in the cake pan and added the stamens. "It means I should've known better than to trust a cop. I'm just an assignment to you."

"You're not *just* an assignment to me," he said firmly. "If I didn't care for you, Amber, I wouldn't be here to discuss this. I wouldn't have come back to help you. If you were *just* an assignment, I would've let the surveillance team handle your safety from here on out. I'd have come and interrupted your workday. I'm here because I *don't* want this to end up just an assignment."

Raw pain showed in her eyes, her actions, even her smile. "Haven't I messed up your life enough, Garrett?"

He stared at her. "Apparently I don't see it that way, or I wouldn't want to talk to you about it."

"You probably know more about me than I do. It wasn't a time of my life I like to remember."

"That's a convenient excuse," he said, trying to understand what she was trying *not* to say. "I don't want to assume that the charges against you tell the entire story. Trust me, I write these reports, so I know I don't often look at crime from the same view as the criminal."

Tears formed in the corners of her eyes.

"I want to know what happened, Amber. It doesn't have to mean it's over…unless that's what you want."

She shook her head. "It's not what I want, but I think it might be best."

"Let's talk," he said. "Then we'll decide together."

Amber closed her eyes, almost as if she was praying, before she said anything. "I had been pretty rebellious in high school, but I think the joy ride and vandalism charges were dropped when I turned eighteen, weren't they?"

"I didn't see them listed, but what were those about?"

"I borrowed my neighbor's car one night. Their son and I had been dating, and the parents didn't approve. So they filed charges. The vandalism charge was when my friends and I tee-peed the football players' houses before homecoming. One kid's dad was a lawyer with no sense of humor."

"And the judge let the charges stick?"

"Someone fell through the roof of his convertible when they jumped out of the tree. Only one person knew who was responsible, and no one confessed, so we were all charged. I didn't do it, but I also didn't stop pushing the limits.

"What you probably read was what happened while I was at school. Mom and Dad wouldn't let me go to the same college as any of my friends, and I was determined to prove I didn't belong there," she said, starting out painfully. "The week before I left for school, I found out that my parents were separating, so off to college I went. By Thanksgiving, I found out from my little sister and brother that it was bitter, and Mom and Dad were in a custody battle. I figured out exactly how to get their attention. I started drinking and missing classes...."

Garrett's legs twitched with the need to move close to her and comfort her, but he forced himself to stay in the straight chair across the coffee table.

"I bought a fake ID so I could...go out and party more." She stopped working and wiped the tears from her eyes. "Then one night I was at a frat party, and the campus cops broke it up. I ran...." Her voice disappeared.

"And they pursued...."

She nodded silently. "You would have thought I was a three-hundred-pound linebacker the way he tackled and cuffed me."

"Was that when you resisted the arrest?"

She shook her head. "That was the second time. It was the same cop, a week later. I hadn't even had a drink yet, but because I was underage and had a cup of beer in my hand, with another fake ID, he was determined to scare some sense into me. He told me stories about girls who were raped, showed me horrible pictures of crimes, and threw me in a freezing-cold jail cell and waited until the end of his shift hours later to let me make a call."

Garrett shook his head. "There's a bad apple in every walk of life, and I'm sorry...."

"You don't have to apologize, Garrett. I know he was out of line, even if his intentions were to protect me. I learned a valuable lesson. A lot of them, actually. I was in with drunk prostitutes all night because Mom and Dad were too busy fighting to answer their phone, bail me out and knock some sense into me like they should have."

"Where'd you go to school again?"

She smiled. "Wyoming, and they probably weren't literally ladies-of-the-evening, but it was about as scary to a nineteen-year-old as if they had been."

"Sounds like you've had some counseling since this all happened."

She shrugged. "Mainly my friend's father, a minister, who agreed to bail me out if I would straighten up and come to services. He's the one who saved me from self-destruction, and I know how blessed I am that he got through to me. Until I ran into you, I was doing pretty well, staying on the right side of the law," she said, the tensing of her jaw betrayed her unrest with the situation.

"Are you still on good terms with your parents?"

She shook her head. "Only as much as I have to be to see my sister and brother. I'm trying to convince my sister how important a college degree really is. I have a skill that hopefully will get me through, but I sometimes regret not going back to school."

"It's never too late."

"One day, maybe, but for now, I'm sure this is where God wants me."

Garrett nodded. "I couldn't agree more." He steepled his hands in front of him and smiled. "Amber, thank you for telling me. Like I said, it sounds nothing like the charges on the report when you explain it."

"I wasn't trying to keep it from you, I just assumed you'd seen it, or maybe I hoped it didn't follow me into Colorado." She glanced at him, then quickly let her gaze drop. "I've heard that you're applying at the FBI, and I'm sure that they wouldn't look favorably on your association with me."

"That's the other issue I wanted to talk to you about. I received letters from two federal agencies that would like me to come for testing next week."

"Congratulations." She forced the word out of her mouth and picked up her decorating bag again.

"Only problem is, I'm not sure it's what God has in mind for me now. And I'm not sure it's what I want anymore."

"You wouldn't have applied if you weren't sure you wanted this opportunity, though."

He leaned forward and drew Amber's attention. "Amber…"

Her eyes flashed with azure fire.

"Things have changed since I sent out the applications three months ago," he said. "If I were offered a job, I would have to go to their academy, and then I probably wouldn't be assigned near here. Three months ago there was no one in my life to keep me from going wherever they needed to send me. Now I have you to think about."

She glanced up, then quickly looked away without a word.

"Would you ever consider relocating?"

Amber dropped the decorating bag and her mouth

fell open. Their gazes met and she teared up again. "Ever is a long time. Most jobs won't leave the offer on the table that long. And I've already told you, my business is here in Fossil Creek…and I think you'd be crazy not to follow through with your dreams. Just like you told me, you can't let anyone else steal them. That includes me."

Garrett pulled Amber close and gazed into her eyes. "What if I told you that you *are* my dream?"

Tears welled in her eyes and she pressed her lips against his. *I'd say I love you, but I can't let you drop out now.* "You've planned all of your life to do this, Garrett. You have to give it your best shot. Maybe we are meant to be together. Maybe that's here, or somewhere else, but…"

"I don't want to walk away from something here, either, and with the way things are changing…"

"I can take care of myself, and you don't need to feel like you have to stay here so I can have my dream. I don't want that, and neither do you. You wouldn't be the same man I love if you gave that up for me."

"Am I wrong to want my cake and eat it, too?"

She laughed. "That's an interesting question from a man who doesn't even like cake."

"As is encouraging me to keep doing a job that you struggle to accept."

SEVENTEEN

Garrett and Amber arrived at the shop bright and early the next morning to fill a small order that Amber had missed when she was making calls after she'd been attacked. She had remembered it at four in the morning, and knocked on his door to let him know she was going to the shop because she had all the ingredients there. The chief agreed to let them work at the shop for a few hours as long as Garrett was there, too.

"You're not going alone," he'd said groggily. "Give me a minute, and I'll be ready to go."

Ten minutes later they were still arguing over her sudden impression that she was safe.

She'd awakened with the determination to show Garrett that she could still fend for herself. It was as if he'd made the decision to move out of state without even informing her. He was quickly learning that arguing with her would only make her more tenacious, and that could be a dangerous thing with a killer on the loose.

Her employees would be joining them fairly early, as they had the bows to finish, cakes to bake and buckets of frosting to mix to take to the resort. Amber was busy making her list and checking it twice, afraid she was going to leave something behind, or worse, totally space out on something she'd agreed to and kill her business. Nervous energy kept her buzzing from one place to the next.

They'd been there only a couple of hours when CiCi called Amber in tears. In addition to the six inches of snow that had fallen overnight, CiCi explained that she'd be late getting to the shop because someone had bashed in the windshield of her car. Garrett called to get the details from the officer on the call, learning that CiCi had left the magnetic signs on the car after she'd finished deliveries a few days ago. "I know it's good advertising under normal circumstances," Garrett said, hoping not to stress anyone out. "But since the shop is closed for a few days, why don't we leave them out of commission for the time being."

While they worked, Garrett called Detective Wang to check on the investigation of Amber's attack. According to him, Melendez had vanished. Garrett struggled to leave the investigation to his fellow officers, but this drive to be involved was getting old. Melendez hadn't left any clues to his whereabouts since he'd attacked Amber.

He still hadn't figured out why Melendez claimed to be after Garrett, yet had run when he'd had the chance to fight. They all supposed it was mainly because Melendez had been surprised to see Garrett. Maybe his hand had slipped off the knife and he knew he couldn't regain his control over Amber, let alone take out Garrett, too. Which meant he probably didn't have a gun.

Nick, Kent and even Dallas had helped get the word

out to gun dealers in the region, warning them about Melendez. Being a narcotics officer, Kent also had some of the seedier eyes watching out for Melendez.

All was fair in love and war. And if he wanted to win the battle of love, he had to lock up the man who'd been building his battle plan for years.

Sean showed up to discuss ideas for the grand re-opening, giving Garrett the opportunity to see if the security company had upgraded the system to include her apartment, as well. "What do you want those flowers for the cake in? I'll start packaging them up."

"Use a couple of sheet-cake boxes, and be sure to use some of the foam in the bottom as a cushion. They're under the display cabinets here," she said, kneeling to pull a couple out. While she told him where to find some foam, Amber folded the boxes and put them together. "Thanks," she said with a kiss on his cheek.

He hurried up to her apartment and started packaging the flowers, mixing the colors on each layer, just as she'd requested. His mind drifted to her apartment, and how he could ease his mind that she would be safe here alone. He knew she was trying to make him believe she could take care of herself. She was a strong woman, but he still didn't want her here alone.

There was no way he could even go for the interviews if they hadn't caught Melendez yet. Unless he could talk Amber into delaying the reopening of the shop until he returned, he needed to reconsider whether this was really what he wanted. Even if they caught the creep, what would he do if they offered him a position?

Half of the flowers were boxed up, and he took a break, going to inspect the handiwork of the security experts. He looked outside, surprised to see Amber slap the magnetic signs to the doors of the rental car and drive off.

He hurried down the stairs. "Where's Amber going?"

Andrea pulled her order book out. "To the student center at the university to deliver…"

Garrett ordered her employees to lock up and not let anyone in, then bolted out the door and into his own car. He called the surveillance team to let them know that while he and Amber were out, there were still three employees in the shop to watch out for.

He drove, but didn't see her anywhere between the shop and the student center building. He was so focused on looking for the red compact with the brightly colored magnetic signs on them that he didn't see the white sedan pull out—causing a domino effect of collisions ahead of him—until it was too late. He screeched to a halt, swerving to miss the other cars, and hit the horn. Two cars going the other direction slid on the ice and collided when they swerved to avoid the white car. He jumped out of the car and wrote down the license number of the car that had caused the collision, then dialed 911.

All four lanes of traffic were blocked. Garrett went into work mode and headed for the damaged vehicle, spotting Amber as she pulled out of the bank parking lot. She hurried off, and suddenly Garrett understood why—the white car that had caused the accident looked like the "patrol" car at the kidnapping.

Amber had dropped off the order for brownies and pastries to the campus women's conference, then had gone by the bank to make a deposit. When she pulled out of the drive-through teller, she heard a horn blaring.

"What'd I do?" she said as she slammed on the brakes and waited for a crash. No one was near her. Down the street, she noticed that a car had pulled out of a parking spot, right in front of another car that was already in the flow of traffic. It was heading in her direction, but far enough away that she had plenty of time to pull out and get out of their way. As it got closer, Amber noticed the car that had nearly caused the crash move to the lane next to her, then drop back behind her again.

It looked a lot like the car that the kidnapper drove. She turned off University Drive and slowed down to see if he would follow.

When she saw him turn, as well, her heart raced. She tried to get a better look at the driver, to see if it was the same guy she'd seen the week before. She couldn't tell for sure. With the icy roads, she was hesitant to speed up, so she slowly headed toward the police station, fishing through her purse for her cell phone. After several blocks he turned.

She wasn't even certain this was Melendez, or simply a coincidence. She dropped her phone back into her purse and decided to head directly back to the shop. Amber realized how stupid it had been to take off without Garrett.

Amber couldn't shake this uneasy feeling. The roads were icy, snow was still coming down and it was getting harder to tell if the car she'd seen was really white, or if her imagination was running rampant. She reconsidered the phone and got it back out of her purse.

The traffic light turned red, and Amber decided it would be wise to call Garrett. *And what do I tell him?* she wondered. She really had no clearer information for him than she'd had before. A white car had followed her for a few blocks—so what?

She had nothing new to help the police catch him, even if it *was* Melendez. Her heart raced, wondering where the car had gone. She was in a quiet residential area, near the college—just like the night of the kidnapping. Amber turned at the next corner to get back on a busy street and away from the solitude. She'd driven several blocks when she noticed an accident ahead of her. "Two pileups within miles of each other. I have got to get back to the shop."

She didn't want to get caught in traffic in the middle of an ice storm where she had no control. Though she felt more comfortable with people around, she didn't like that traffic building up behind her. *Too late now.* She slowed down and looked for a way out. Finally she cleared Garrett's number and entered 911. She put the car in Park, turned it off and pressed the send button to report the traffic accident. Suddenly her car door flew open.

Melendez grabbed her arm and tugged. With his other hand, he pulled a knife out of his pocket, flipped the blade out and held it to her throat. "Get out peacefully, or this time it won't be just a scratch."

Amber prayed that he hadn't seen her cell phone, and while she pretended to be reaching for the seat belt, she dropped her phone into her coat pocket and grabbed the steering wheel. "What makes you think I'd go with you, Melendez?"

He paused, then tightened his grip.

"Yeah, Garrett knows it's you. All of the cops know you. Now you have all the Matthews men after you." She held on tight, hoping to buy enough time that someone in the crowd would notice and do something.

"Shut up," he growled, switching the knife to his right hand and pulling a small taser from his belt with the other. He cut the seat belt in one swipe and wrestled her out of the car with such force that she felt as if he'd dislocated her wrists.

She struggled to get her feet under her, but the ground was too slick, and he was moving too quickly. She watched her rental car and her purse get farther away, and onlookers simply stared.

She twisted, hoping he'd drop her. "You're a bully. No one wants you, so you force yourself…"

He repeated his order and kept dragging her into the alley, ignoring the police officer who ordered him to stop from some fifty yards away.

"Let her go."

He walked backward to keep her between the gun and himself.

"Where are you going? Same place you took Jenna Miller? You didn't know her name when you kidnapped her, did you? She has a name. Jenna. And a boyfriend." There was no way to get her grip on this ice to try to pull loose. Plus, if she fought too hard, he might just use the knife now.

She wanted to live. *God, please don't let him kill me. Give me strength.*

Sirens whistled, and he hurried to open the door of the police car. A real one this time. He slammed her against the car, jabbed her with the taser and she felt the electric current jolt her, just as it had Jenna. She tried to be strong. Tried to fight back, and waited for it to stop long enough for her to run, or kick him.

She had to try something. It kept going, and felt her legs weakening.

The electric current stopped and he grabbed her wrist, slapping a handcuff on her. She couldn't fight back.

"Where'd you get this police car?" she said, hoping her phone was still connected to 911, hoping they could hear her.

"You have a death wish…" he said, right before calling her another vulgar name and tasing her again. "When are you going to get it? Your boyfriend took my life—I'm taking his. His life, his car, his girl." He made another disgusting promise, and she hoped she died before having to live through it.

She tried to move, but he held her tight. Then she felt herself sliding across the hard plastic seat in the back of a cop car. She didn't care how dirty it was or how she was locked back there, she just wanted him to leave her alone.

She thanked God that the guy and the taser were on the other side of the metal cage. Finally she'd have a chance to catch her breath. *If Sarah, as petite as she is, can survive this, so can I,* she thought.

Her mind wandered to the night before, when she and Garrett had visited for several hours. It was enough to make her realize how much she cared about him and wanted him in her life. She knew she should be happier that he was getting the opportunity of a lifetime to be a federal agent, but in her heart, she hoped that he would stay in Fossil Creek.

She still felt blue from telling Garrett that she wouldn't relocate with him—now she thought it sounded wonderful. But how was she supposed to respond to something like that? Wasn't it far too early in their relationship to make any promises?

Garrett had just pulled away from the accident as the police arrived. He paused next to the officer and said that he'd be able to explain later—he had to look for the car that had caused this accident.

He called the chief and explained what had happened, and he was looking for Amber. He paused at each intersection, hoping he'd see some sign that she had been there. He'd seen her turn off the main drag a mile or so down the road, and guessed at the exact street she had taken.

"She's strong willed, I'll give her that," the chief said. "Keep me informed."

Garrett could only imagine what the chief had wanted to say. He put his phone away and made a few more rounds of the area before giving up. He was almost at the shop when his phone rang again. He didn't even get to answer before the chief interrupted him.

"We just had a police car stolen, Garrett. A block away, the white vehicle with the stolen plates that you called in was found, empty. So it's likely that he's in one of our cars, where we can track him with the GPS system."

"We missed him again?"

"Not only that, there is a second pileup on University Avenue, at Mountain Lane. Amber's car is abandoned there. Witnesses saw Melendez pull her out of the car at knifepoint."

Garrett couldn't believe what he was hearing. "What—" He started to speak, but the chief interrupted him.

"That's right."

"You're sure it's Amber?" But he knew no one on the force would make any assumptions of identity if they weren't sure.

"Yes, we're sure. She called 911 for something, but we don't know for sure why, and we still have her on the line."

"What do you mean, you don't know why? What'd she say?"

"She's said plenty, identifying Melendez, said your name, that's how I figured out who it was. He's kidnapped her. He has the police car, stolen from the accident just up University Avenue, where he left the white car there in the bank parking lot. Our GPS network is tracking him, as well, but we presume he's smart enough to figure out that we'll find him faster in that than any other car. So I figure he's going to abandon it as soon as he finds another available vehicle. The telephone company is working to get a location for us before we lose him in the car. Sit tight."

"Call my cell if you find out anything," Garrett insisted. "I'm going to be at her shop, in case he calls there."

"You think he will?" the chief asked.

"According to what he told Amber the night he was in her apartment, I'm sure of it. I'm just praying he'll be reasonable, and not hurt Amber."

The chief paused. "Finish up there, and then get to the station. If he calls, I want you to have backup and all of the information we can pull together."

"Sounds good. I'll see you in a while," Garrett said. He pulled into the alley, hoping Melendez would have brought her back to the shop to negotiate. No such luck. He went inside, and the chatter stopped instantly. Andrea turned off the mixer. Sean set down the pan he was greasing.

"Where's Amber?"

"She's been kidnapped," he said flatly. "Feel free to eavesdrop when I call my family. I can't go through it more than once, then I need to get to the station in case he calls there for a…" He only hoped Melendez would keep her alive as a bargaining chip. He looked at the boxes of wedding decorations, then at the terrified faces staring at him.

"All this because she witnessed a crime?" CiCi said bitterly.

Garrett didn't have time to argue, or explain, whichever CiCi was trying to do. "If he shows up, you get out of here and call the police. I know we're in the middle of this wedding, so unless you're too upset to keep working, continue as if nothing has happened. I'll have my brothers both come over to keep an eye out for Melendez."

Garrett plugged in his cell phone to charge, then used the landline to call his family and explain what had happened. The chief had already thought to send

Nick over, but suggested sending Sarah, as support for Amber, and to let Melendez think she was less of a threat than two male officers.

After he'd finished making the calls, he looked at her employees, who were as afraid to voice their silent fears as he was.

"Should I call the bride and tell her Amber can't…"

"No, you shouldn't. Don't even think it. I'm getting her back," Garrett insisted.

"Okay," CiCi squeaked. "How long until I should call her? She has…"

"I don't know," he said. "When I find something out, where's the information to reach the bride?"

"Amber has the book. Or did…"

"Oh," Garrett said. "Look and see if she left it here somewhere. I'll have my mom look at the house. I don't want to call her grandmother yet. If you need to reach me, for any reason at all, here's my cell number." He snatched up the cell phone along with the cord, and walked back out to his car. He didn't want to deal with compassionate people right now. He needed to be out there, finding Amber.

He and a team of officers and detectives had been in constant contact all day. It was crazy in town. A record-setting blizzard was bearing down on the city, everyone was frantic to get to wherever they were going and no one seemed to remember how to drive on icy roads.

"What do you remember about this guy, Gar?" his brother Kent asked. He had come to offer manpower. "He's not anyone I've heard of."

"Try Spider Melendez," his dad said as he walked

into the room. "It was a long time ago, but that might explain why he's not showing up. I think his father was killed in a drive-by gang shooting in 1997. His uncle tried to help him, but he wanted nothing of it."

"So he wasn't in the gang during the Explorers?"

"No, but he wasn't in the club for the right reasons. He wanted to learn to shoot and take out the gang that killed his dad. Oddly enough, if I remember correctly, he finally got 'Chains' in Amarillo and ended up in prison in Texas, and joined one of the prison gangs."

One of the officers scrambled to get the information, and there it was. "He legally changed his name when he was released in 2007. His lawyer got him out on good behavior."

Garrett was overwhelmed with information. "So where would he go now? Where'd his parents live? He hasn't been downtown, which is where I'd have gone if I were insane."

Kent slapped his back, then squeezed his shoulder, none of which Garrett could feel through the Kevlar vest. "We'll find her, Gar."

"I want her now, alive and…"

"We know," his dad said sympathetically.

Garrett rested his forehead on his hands and closed his eyes. He didn't know what else to do but pray. *Take care of Amber, Father. Be her guardian and protector. Shield her from Melendez's evil. Give her strength, Lord, and wrap Your arms around her. Let her know that we're looking, that I love her and I won't stop until I've rescued her.*

Twenty minutes later the police car was located with the GPS and computer ripped out. What he didn't understand was that it would be useless to him outside the car. Nevertheless, it was also useless to them, since the wires had been cut.

"Any other cars reported missing since the kidnapping?" Fingers tapped on the keyboard as the investigator ran a query.

"Where did they find the car?" his dad asked.

"Northridge High."

"Fifteen years ago that was a housing development, and close to where the kid's family lived. A couple of the houses left out there are now used by the school for storage. Find out what Tony Melendez's previous address was."

"How do I find that out?"

"Ask his uncle. Lieutenant Chavez."

Garrett and his dad rode with Kent in his unmarked beat-up narc car, and the chief ordered the SWAT team to head out there. It was only a couple of minutes until they heard back from Chavez, who said he'd been looking for his nephew since his release, but hadn't found Anthony yet.

"Why didn't you tell me Chavez was Melendez's uncle? He's probably been covering for him all along."

His dad shook his head. "Not Chavez. He did everything he could to straighten the kid out. He's probably been working double time to try to figure out where he's hiding." They each had their full gear, but were in plainclothes.

As they passed the abandoned police car, Garrett watched for footprints. They headed directly toward the outer buildings of the school. "I'm not waiting for the SWAT team," Garrett warned. "So if you want…"

"We're right behind you, Gar," both men said at the same time.

Sure enough, there was a window broken out of one of the buildings, and drag marks to it. It would have been a long walk from the police car in this weather.

His dad was first to the door to provide cover. Kent kicked it in, and Garrett rushed in first.

Amber was huddled in the corner by some boxes, but Melendez was nowhere to be found. Garrett threw the boxes aside and pulled Amber to her feet. She'd been gagged and tied up, but at least she still had her coat on and looked to be okay.

Garrett wrapped her in his arms and held her close. "Are you okay?"

She nodded. "Just scared. It smells in here, Garrett. Get me out of here."

He sniffed. "Kent, Dad, look around. I think Amber's found a decomposed body."

He took her out to Kent's car. "Do you want to get in? Are you warm enough?"

"I'll be fine, Garrett. It's just good to have some fresh air and to be safe. I heard gunshots a while ago. I heard two men yelling, and then it got quiet."

The SWAT team searched the rest of the buildings, finding Melendez, with his gun in his hand and a bullet through his head.

Before they took Amber home, she would need to see the body, in case it was Jenna Miller. "Later," Garrett said.

"But…"

"Send pictures," Garrett insisted. "She's been smelling the body for hours—I'm not about to make her go back in there."

Kent and his dad joined Amber and Garrett, leaving the detectives to process the scene. As they discussed the case, Garrett took hold of Amber's hand, thanking God for answering their prayers.

Amber closed her eyes and said a prayer that this wasn't the woman she'd seen kidnapped that night. She didn't want to be the last person to have seen Jenna Miller alive.

When Kent stopped the car, Garrett escorted her into the police station. He wrapped his arms around her and held her tight.

"Hi," Nick said. "Good to see you."

"Thanks," she said to Nick, then looked at Garrett. "Do I have to look…?"

"Just pictures for now," Garrett confirmed. "That should be enough, I hope. It looks like she's been dead for a few days."

Amber felt her breakfast threaten to come up. "Could I get some water, please?"

Nick escorted her down the hall, while Garrett disappeared to get her something to drink. He opened a door and motioned for her to go on inside. "Garrett will be back in a few minutes and Detective Wang should be here pretty soon. Have you eaten recently? I could get you some crackers if you're not feeling well."

"That might help. Breakfast was a long time ago." But about now she was wondering if eating would be a good thing. She found herself praying she wouldn't get sick all over the interrogation room and make a fool of herself.

Another officer followed them into the cold, stale room, and said, "go ahead and have a seat."

She looked at the dingy chair and unsightly walls, remembering the door of the jail cell that had closed behind her. "Wait," she said, her heart pounding and her breathing quicker than normal. She didn't want to sit in here alone. "Where's Garrett?"

"He'll be right back," the officer said, blocking the doorway. Whether it was to keep her from leaving the claustrophobia-prone room, or to show her that he was still in charge, Amber couldn't tell. Just then, Sarah Roberts walked into the room. "I'll wait with Ms. Scott." She was so short, she had to look up to Amber. "If that's okay?"

Amber nodded, and the other officer let the door close. She glanced at Sarah, still in awe that someone so petite could hold her own as a cop. Sarah offered a hug and Amber felt tears stream down her face.

Sarah walked to the table and pulled out the chair. "Try to relax. This is much less traumatic than going to the morgue," she said gently, then filled Amber in on what to expect from the photos. "Think of it as a scene from a television show and it's a little easier. Go ahead and make yourself comfortable."

Amber lowered herself into the chair, careful not to touch anything, as it didn't look terribly clean. "Does it ever bother you?"

"Only when I let myself get attached…." Before they could continue the conversation, two men crowded into the room, Garrett following them both. He handed her a bottle of water, and the older man introduced himself as Chief Thomas and the other man as Detective Wang.

"Ms. Scott," Detective Wang said with a nod. He then reviewed the specifics of Amber's report and asked her to verify that she was the same person who witnessed the incident. Once she verbally confirmed, he continued. "We've identified the body of Jenna Miller based upon the yellow sport utility vehicle that you identified."

Detective Wang articulated the details of the case, as known at this point, anyway. Amber wondered if that was because he'd never contacted her before, or if this was common. Or…she stole a look at Garrett.

She hadn't seen him in uniform since the night of their accident and liked the reminder of her first impression of him—when he'd captured her heart.

"Ms. Scott," he reiterated, as if he knew her mind was wandering. "Is this the woman you saw that evening?" He pulled photographs out of the folder. "Take your time—there's no rush."

She took a sip of the water Garrett had brought her and glanced at him standing across the room facing her. He looked irresistibly handsome in his navy blue pants and shirt. The corner of his mouth twitched, and she felt as if he was trying to shield her from the shock of looking at photographs of Jenna Miller.

She inhaled deeply and let it out, then looked at the photos. Each one had been taken from a different angle. The lighting was so different from that night and it was hard to tell for sure if the woman's hair had been this red at sunset. Would it look darker in the lower light? Was this the woman Amber had been determined to find?

"It might be her. I'm not sure. Do you have other pictures of her...alive, I mean?"

"What isn't right?" Garrett asked.

She looked at him. "Her hair is so red here. But it's probably the sunlight. It looked darker and browner that night."

Detective Wang jotted notes on a pad of paper. "I'll see if her family can bring some pictures when they come, but for now, this is all we have to go on."

"She looks so pale and puffy," Amber said, staring at Jenna's face.

"It's normal postmortem."

She wondered if she could have stopped this from ending this way. Amber wiped at her forehead and then covered her mouth. She looked at Jenna's clothing. "I'm pretty sure it's the same woman I saw kidnapped. I recognize her shirt." Details of that night flashed through her mind. It seemed a lifetime ago.

Garrett cleared his throat. "Can we get onto today's incident?"

"Sure. Ms. Scott, would you identify this man, for the record?"

"I don't know him. Who is he?"

Detective Wang stared at her. "This isn't the man who kidnapped you or Jenna Miller? Or the man who broke in to your apartment?"

The room went silent and Amber felt as if she was remembering things totally wrong. "No, I've never seen him before."

Garrett looked at the photo. "This isn't the man from her apartment. So it looks like he has an accomplice."

"Had an accomplice. Let's hope he's the only one. Find out who this is, ASAP, and be sure to check for any gang ties." Detective Wang handed the photo to an officer, then focused again on his notes. "So, Ms. Scott, go through everything as it happened today."

She went through the events, clarifying questions as the detective wrote things down. By the time she got to the end, nothing seemed real. "And when did the suspect take your cell phone from you?"

"When he stopped to disable the computer. He couldn't get it to turn off. That's when he asked if I had a phone. I told him I thought I'd dropped it in the car. He yanked me out of the car and threw me against it…" She tried to get the image out of her head.

"What did he do?" Wang asked quietly. "Did he frisk you?"

She nodded. "After he tased me."

"He tased you before frisking you?"

She was breathing faster. "I'd tried to get away, and that's when he tased me. I finally figured out that he liked it when I fought him. It was like he was living out some fantasy or something. So I told him where the phone was, and he took it and drove in the opposite direction, then took out the battery and drove over the cell phone."

"Any idea where that was?" Wang asked.

"We were on that back highway between Fossil Creek and Bondurant. He kept calling someone, asking if the coast was clear. It wasn't very far, but with the bad roads, I was afraid we were going to slide off the road and die."

There was a long silence, as the officers looked to

Wang for the next question. "When you heard the suspect talking to the other person, did you recognize the voice?"

"Not that I recall. It was a man with a deep voice."

"Can you give us any impressions of the relationship between the two?"

"They talked about covering each other's backs, like they'd been close friends who helped each other through a tough time."

"Now? Or at some other time?" Wang clarified.

"Both," she answered. "Oh, and the second guy said they needed to take out his uncle. I didn't realize at the time who that was, but Melendez said he'd take care of him, not to worry about that."

The chief whispered to Nick, then Nick left the room in a hurry.

"Did you hear anything else?"

"I heard sirens, and a car. Then there was one gunshot, and then Garrett and his dad and brother broke in to the building I was in, and then a few minutes later there was another round of shots, and then Garrett took me outside because of the smell."

"After the one shot, you're sure there wasn't another vehicle?"

"I was focused on the sirens, just hoping the police were coming to get me. Sorry."

"Ms. Scott, I understand you live alone. Do you have somewhere else you can stay for a while?"

"I'm staying with friends right now," she said, uncertain whether she should tell who exactly.

The chief shook his head, motioning for Sarah and Detective Wang to leave. After the door closed behind them, he waved his hand at the two-way mirror. "Ms.

Scott. The other day I assigned Officer Matthews to provide twenty-four-hour surveillance. I appreciate your cooperation. I'm sure it has been a hardship closing down the shop for a few days, but I need to ask you to remain closed while we make sure we have the right man behind bars."

"But the shop has a new security alarm." She looked at Garrett, wondering why he hadn't told her about the chief's change in plan. "I can't just close down my business."

"Unless you'd like to end up—" the chief started to say, but Garrett interrupted him.

"I'm sure my parents would be willing to let her stay with them as long as necessary. I could bring her in at two or three in the morning, and help her, while providing…"

"No," she said before thinking clearly. "Thank you, but no, I have to do this on my own."

"There's no way I'm going to let you keep endangering yourself and your employees," Garrett argued. "We take care of our own, Chief, and the same applies to those we love. And you may as well know now, I plan to convince Amber to marry me, sooner or later—her choice."

Amber stared at him in disbelief. He was probably the most honorable man she'd ever known. She couldn't let him risk his job like this.

"Aren't you going to—" the chief began to ask.

"I'm not going to test with the federal agencies."

The chief paced the room, then ordered Detective Wang to get in there. No one moved. "Good, they cut the speakers." He leaned his hands on the table and glared at Amber. "What I started to say is, aren't you going to give Matthews an answer?"

Her lip quivered. "Yes, sir, I will."

"You will? He risks his job, his entire career, and you can only say you will? You're a wedding planner and you—"

"I mean I will give him an answer, but not in the middle of an interrogation room in a police station."

The chief let out an unexpected chuckle. "You are aware that because of officer safety, part of his employment hinges on an interview of a potential spouse, don't you?"

"It stands to reason. I've already told him that I'm a liability for his career goals." She looked at Garrett and smiled.

The chief did, too. He looked from Amber to Garrett and back. "I've known the Matthews family for decades and I don't think I could recommend marriage to a better man." He went through the reality of a cop's life and marriage, divorce rates, stress and the importance of having a support network.

Amber wasn't swayed. "If I was going to give up when the going gets tough, I would never have taken over my grandmother's business in Old Town. Stress is only negative if you don't have someone in your life who can make you laugh, even in the middle of troubling times."

"Take your fiancée back to her shop to get her things, Garrett. Amber, I don't want to unjustly scare you, but from all the evidence we've seen, I do believe there's reason for taking these precautions."

"Why?" Amber said eyeing Garrett. "What makes you think…"

"I don't believe the vandalism of CiCi's car was a random incident."

"How'd you know about that?"

She expected some glib remark, but was surprised when he admitted that he'd been watching her, even when she thought he'd gone home for the night. "When I saw you leave to make deliveries, Sean told me something had happened to CiCi's car, that you'd taken the last set of magnetic signs. I called dispatch and got the details."

She thought back to CiCi's phone call. After that, she'd noticed the car following her. "Why would he go after CiCi? And why wouldn't he have come after me immediately?"

"Until this week, Parties Galore only existed on your van. It was in the shop. The bakery is still listed and advertised under the previous name, until your new sign was put up. So now that you have the magnetic signs, and have the new sign, it's possible that the suspect believes he's now found the witness. I don't think Melendez associated you with the case until the new sign went up. I think he was after you to hurt me."

Amber let out a gasp.

The chief stood with his arms crossed over his chest. "Could be trying to make sure he has the right person, but that would mean he actually has a conscience. We haven't found any similar profile between his victims or pattern to his crimes. And I don't plan on letting one develop."

"I suspect he's inflicting the same torment that he's been through, knowing that someone can identify him.

Vandalizing CiCi's car was a message that he's found you. Then, this morning, he made sure you knew he was there. He drove the same car so you'd recognize it. He pulled up next to you, then dropped back."

"How'd you know that?" she asked.

"I was the truck he almost ran into as you came out of the bank drive-through. I'm not about to let him get to you again, Amber."

Garrett moved to calm her down.

"We can't tell you any more details than this, Amber," the chief said. "I know you've had your doubts that we've been investigating this, but I assure you, it was never ignored. I'm sorry we couldn't tell you more. And now, thanks to Garrett's professional expertise, and his personal commitment to assure your safety, we know who we're looking for, and we will catch him—sooner than later."

"I don't think he's going to strike like he has with the others, which I still believe were crimes of opportunity. Now his rage is going to escalate because you're his first specific target. We can catch him, Amber, but I need you to trust us and do everything exactly as we say." His gaze met hers and she felt her anxiety fade just knowing Garrett was going to be taking care of her.

"I can't close the shop, not completely," she said, trying to sound stronger than she felt. She felt little more than desperation. "You know that. I have a big wedding this weekend, and…"

"I know this isn't going to be easy for you to give up being in charge, Amber." Garrett put his hands on her shoulders and looked her in the eye. "Don't worry. I have a plan to get you to the wedding on time."

EIGHTEEN

Garrett had changed out of his police uniform, prepared to go back undercover as a bakery employee until they caught Anthony "Spider" Melendez, the kid that had been kicked out of the police Explorers group in high school. The kid that the SWAT officer killed was one of Melendez's gang affiliates in prison. They still hadn't been able to find any evidence that he belonged, as well.

He just had a grudge to settle with the local police department because of his uncle, Lieutenant Chavez and the Matthews men. He thought he had finally found a way to get revenge on all of them.

After they left the station, Garrett took Amber to the shop to pack some clothes, and to get whatever else she needed to finish up for the wedding. "While you pack, I'll check my messages."

Her mind wasn't on the incident or on her obligations. "You weren't really serious, were you?"

"Serious about what?"

"About what? What do you think?"

"Oh," he said with a smile. "Of course I was serious. I wasn't thinking about how it would come across, clearly, but I did want my intentions to be clear, to the chief, and to you. So you have time to consider your answer, but I assure you, I will ask again."

"You are never going to live down proposing in the middle of an interrogation," she said with a chuckle. "That had better not be…"

"That wasn't meant to be the official proposal, but I didn't want to leave the chief in the dark. He needs to know my plans. So you do have time to think about it. I'll make it up to you, I promise." He reached across the console in between their seats and took hold of her hand.

"I thought I made that clear. I don't care about that stuff. God has shown me what true love is, Garrett. I'd marry you tonight if it weren't for this case, but I want to remember God joining you and me as one and being able to celebrate that every year without remembering running away from a criminal. I want everyone to know I didn't marry you just because you were my very handsome bodyguard."

"We know the truth, and that's really all we need to worry about."

She gazed at him as he concentrated on the road. "I've tried to convince myself not to fall in love with you. I knew I should tell you it was nothing so you could reach for your dreams, but I couldn't…and then you turned and proposed to me.

"My family told me that I'd never find true love because I wanted the perfect courtship. And while I was busy chasing my dreams God brought me the least romantic and the most loving, giving, forgiving and selfless man to capture my heart."

"Who says I'm not romantic? I haven't had a chance to prove myself yet."

"That's just it, Garrett. "I'm hired to create the illusion of perfect romance for weddings, and yet you've shown me that when love is real, you don't need to spend a penny to set the scene. That's the gift God has given me every time you walk into my life."

They arrived at the shop, and Garrett locked the doors and set the security again. They walked into the shop and Amber instantly shifted gears, back to the focused party planner that he loved.

"I'm supposed to head up to the resort with the decorations and cake tomorrow. Do you think they finished baking the cake? I have to pick up the rental van, return the car, oh, where is the car?"

"Don't worry about the rental car tonight. Dad and I will come tomorrow with my folks' van and we'll take the scenic way out of town so Melendez doesn't follow us. I think you should call your employees to let them know you're okay and that the shop will be closed for a while. I'll help you finish the cake today. I'll help cover your normal weekend sales, but I don't see any reason to risk…"

"I know," she said, biting the words off, as if she was trying to hold back her irritation. She took a deep breath and closed her eyes. "I know you're right. Just let me sort through all of this." She glanced at her answering machine and listened to the messages—the most urgent one from the bride—they had to postpone the wedding because they had three feet of snow at the resort. Amber quickly dialed Maya to reassure her that she'd be ready whenever, the delay wasn't a problem for Parties Galore.

She moved to get a suitcase out of her closet and Garrett panicked. "Amber…" He pulled her into his arms and kissed her slowly.

"Well, there's no rush to do all of this now. Just take enough so you can get some sleep. And pack light. Do you have one of those giant purses that will hold everything but the kitchen sink?"

She laughed. "Yeah, I think I can find one."

"We need to leave, Amber. We'll be back in the morning to finish up all of this. You have your staff's phone numbers and addresses? Just to be sure this guy doesn't try to threaten any of them, like he did CiCi, maybe we should send officers to get them, as well."

"You don't think…"

Garrett pulled out his cell phone and dialed Nick. "We're ready," he said, then disconnected and turned back to Amber. "We're not dealing with a reasonable person. We'll call the police with their addresses on the way to my parents and…"

Amber hurried into the office and returned with a file folder and put it into her bag, then went to turn out the lights.

"Leave them on. We want it to look like we're here. Nick is going to be by in a few minutes with Sarah, and I'd like it to look like we're just out on a double date."

There was a knock on the door and Garrett reached for the doorknob.

"Sounds like Nick and Sarah are here."

"I'm feeling like I'm going to vanish into thin air, like witness protection or…"

Garrett opened the door and Anthony Melendez

rushed inside, a gun in one hand, and a taser in the other. He smiled at Garrett.

"Remember me, Garrett? I've been waiting a long time to settle the score."

NINETEEN

Garrett pushed himself in front of Amber, staying between her and Melendez. She wrapped her hand around his waist, holding him close. He was still wearing his bulletproof vest. She felt for his gun, but it wasn't in his holster where it had been the other night.

"You still trying to play cop, I see, Melendez. I hate to tell you, you never will have what it takes to wear a real badge."

"Keep your hands up, Garrett. Just step out of the way. I came for the party planner." A shot rang out and hit one of the stainless-steel bowls sitting on the shelf. "You don't have to have a badge to learn to use a gun."

"It takes more than a gun to be a cop, Melendez. Ask your cousins about that. But then again, even the gang rejected you, didn't they?"

"I've never been part of any gang."

"That's why you wanted to be a cop, because you didn't have what it took to fit in there, either. Nobody wanted little Tony Melendez."

What was Garrett doing, taunting the creep? Amber felt something jab her rib. "God is a shield to all who take refuge in Him," she whispered. "God, be our shield."

"Took this sham of a department long enough to even figure out that I was the one outsmarting all of their educated idiots. Lot of good that degree in criminal justice is going to do you now, smart boy. I had you all convinced this was gangsters territory, blaming them. When this is over, they'll take over the war on cops."

Nick beeped the horn in the alley and Melendez turned to push the door closed. Sarah stood in the way, her gun pointing right at him. "I wouldn't even think about it."

"Give it up, Melendez," Garrett said, pointing a gun at the guy's head. "I'm not about to give you the satisfaction of suicide by officer. You're going to prison. Justice for all of your victims."

Melendez lifted his gun to his head and a shot rang out. The guy swore, then clutched his bloody hand to his body. "I'll make you pay, Matthews."

"I think you have that turned around, Tony." Garrett slipped back into cop mode, reading Anthony Melendez his Miranda rights and efficiently putting the handcuffs on him.

TWENTY

Two days later, Amber and Garrett were standing in the mountain resort with the high glass wall overlooking the ski slopes. He admired the white snow glistening behind the pastel hibiscus-covered wedding cake.

"You couldn't have planned a more beautiful backdrop," Garrett said, wrapping his arms around her shoulders. "You, me and the Lord."

"It's just too bad the wedding party didn't make it up here because of the snow," she said with a smile. "I can't believe they were snowed out twice."

"Let's not waste a perfectly beautiful cake. The pastor's upstairs in his hotel room, and I'm sure we could drum up a few witnesses to make it legal."

"You have to be the most romantic cop I've ever fallen in love with, Garrett."

He smiled. "What do you think? Care to become Mrs. Matthews today?"

"Keep joking around, and I might just say yes."

"I can't think of anything that would make me any happier than to ask the Lord to bless this day as our wedding anniversary." He turned her around to face him and kissed her softly on the lips. "I love you, Amber."

She saw the tenderness in his eyes. "I love you, Garrett, but the bride and groom should be able to make it up here by tomorrow morning. They'll want their cake."

"They can keep the cake. I just want the party planner."

She laughed. "As long as I can have the bodyguard," she said. "Today's a perfect day for a wedding."

* * * * *

Dear Reader,

Shield of Refuge has been a long time in planning, and sometimes the more we plan, the more determined God is to get us to slow down and listen to His plan. Garrett thinks he has his life all planned out, until Amber's determination to find the truth places her life in jeopardy. He's determined to escape falling in love, but the minute he meets Amber all his plans are turned upside down.

I love hearing how different the experiences of falling in love is for every couple. Writing romance probably sounds pretty simple—formulaic, even. Despite claims of dating services, I don't believe there is a scientific, logical or perfect formula for finding one's soul mate. Not even in fiction. So when Garrett and Amber fell in love at first sight, it ruined my plotting, over and over. These two were absolutely determined they were going to call the shots. They had their "plans," and they didn't like having roadblocks thrown in their way. And as determined as they were to follow all the rules of their own plans, they were forced to turn their lives to God, the author of perfect happily-ever-afters.

I do hope you've enjoyed all the IN THE LINE OF FIRE books, where the Matthews siblings put on the armor of God to fight drugs, assault and corruption every day.

If you'd like to contact me, write carol@carolsteward.com, or P.O. Box 200286, Evans, CO 80620.

Carol Steward

QUESTIONS FOR DISCUSSION

1. Amber has several reactions when she sees the officer take the girl away. How easy would it be in a crisis to step into a situation that could put you in danger? Do you think that it is instinctive for people to be brave?

2. One of Amber's roadblocks to helping the victim is her personal fear and bias toward the police. Most of us, at one time or another, have the opportunity to question our own prejudices. What are some of the situations you have been in where you've been forced to take a stand? How did it turn out?

3. Garrett is also put to the test, personally and professionally. Do you think it is his personal strength or his faith in God that presses him to keep looking for the truth even though his boss implies that he shouldn't? Have you ever been in a situation where you needed to disagree with or blatantly ignore someone in authority? How did you come to terms with taking the action that you did?

4. As time goes on and no one has been reported missing, Amber begins to believe that she was seeing things. Have you ever had experiences when you see something totally different than someone else?

5. Amber and Garrett meet in a very unique way, and react to their situation in ways that surprise even themselves. She expects to be afraid of all cops, and he thinks he is going to resent her, yet their reactions are totally opposite. Do you ever surprise yourself with how you react to a situation or individual?

6. Amber has a difficult time forgiving herself for mistakes that she made in her life and makes the assumption that Garrett will also be unwilling to overlook her mistakes. How does Garrett's response demonstrate God's love for each of us?

7. Garrett is very goal oriented, and has a career plan all set out until his run-in with Amber makes him take another look at this plan. Do you ever feel that God puts hurdles up for us to slow us down so we have time to reconsider what His plan is for us? When a door closes in front of you, do you look at it as failure, or opportunity for growth?

8. Amber faced some huge challenges in her young adulthood that forced her to change the course of her life. Have you, or someone you know, had to get over some difficult hurdles in life, and how did you get over them?

9. Garrett sets his mind on something and doesn't easily let it go. Amber is also very strong willed. How can two individuals overcome what could be a constant battle in a marriage?

10. Amber finds it difficult to understand the reason Garrett won't tell her why he thinks she's in danger. Have you ever found it difficult to trust someone else? How do we learn to trust?

11. Amber's and Garrett's lives have crossed paths several times, and yet they wouldn't have met had it not been for God's perfect timing. One minute's difference and the accident would never have happened. Think about a "coincidence" in your life, and how God's timing played a role.

12. Amber and Garrett want to fall in love, but they don't want it to interrupt the plans for their lives. When our wants conflict with our needs, something has to give. Have you ever felt God leading you one way or another? How can we hear God answering our prayers for guidance? Is that "revelation" always the same?

13. Garrett has the chance to seek revenge on the suspect, and yet he doesn't. Why do you think he doesn't? What do you think you would have done if you had been in his shoes?

14. Amber reacts in fear when she witnesses the crime. By the end of the book, when she's had time to think through it all, do you think if she faced a similar situation she would react differently?

REQUEST YOUR FREE BOOKS!

2 FREE RIVETING INSPIRATIONAL NOVELS
PLUS 2 FREE MYSTERY GIFTS

Love Inspired
SUSPENSE

YES! Please send me 2 FREE Love Inspired® Suspense novels and my 2 FREE mystery gifts (gifts are worth about $10). After receiving them, if I don't wish to receive any more books, I can return the shipping statement marked "cancel". If I don't cancel, I will receive 4 brand-new novels every month and be billed just $4.24 per book in the U.S. or $4.74 per book in Canada, plus 25¢ shipping and handling per book and applicable taxes, if any*. That's a savings of over 20% off the cover price! I understand that accepting the 2 free books and gifts places me under no obligation to buy anything. I can always return a shipment and cancel at any time. Even if I never buy another book, the two free books and gifts are mine to keep forever.   123 IDN ERXX 323 IDN ERXM

Name	(PLEASE PRINT)	
Address		Apt. #
City	State/Prov.	Zip/Postal Code

Signature (if under 18, a parent or guardian must sign)

Order online at www.LoveInspiredSuspense.com
Or mail to Steeple Hill Reader Service:
IN U.S.A.: P.O. Box 1867, Buffalo, NY 14240-1867
IN CANADA: P.O. Box 609, Fort Erie, Ontario L2A 5X3

Not valid to current subscribers of Love Inspired Suspense books.

**Want to try two free books from another series?
Call 1-800-873-8635 or visit www.morefreebooks.com**

* Terms and prices subject to change without notice. N.Y. residents add applicable sales tax. Canadian residents will be charged applicable provincial taxes and GST. Offer not valid in Quebec. This offer is limited to one order per household. All orders subject to approval. Credit or debit balances in a customer's account(s) may be offset by any other outstanding balance owed by or to the customer. Please allow 4 to 6 weeks for delivery. Offer available while quantities last.

> **Your Privacy:** Steeple Hill Books is committed to protecting your privacy. Our Privacy Policy is available online at www.SteepleHill.com or upon request from the Reader Service. From time to time we make our lists of customers available to reputable third parties who may have a product or service of interest to you. If you would prefer we not share your name and address, please check here. ☐

LISUS08R

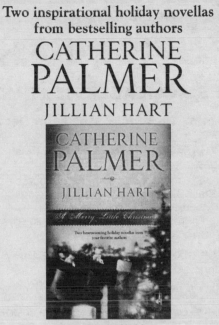

Love Inspired.
SUSPENSE

TITLES AVAILABLE NEXT MONTH

Don't miss these four stories in December

DOUBLE THREAT CHRISTMAS by Terri Reed
The McClains

She had means, motive, opportunity—of course
Megan McClain is accused of double homicide. But Megan
isn't willing to spend Christmas in jail for a crime she didn't
commit. And nothing Detective Paul Wallace says will stop
her from finding the killer herself—at any cost.

SEASON OF GLORY by Ron and Janet Benrey
Cozy Mystery

Why would anyone poison a holiday tea party?
Andrew Ballantine knows his would-be killer is still
in Glory, North Carolina. And to thwart the culprit,
he'll have to get well. Which means letting lovely nurse
Sharon Pickard closer than he'd like....

SUSPICION by Ginny Aiken
Carolina Justice

When Stephanie Scott is mugged, longtime admirer Sheriff
Hal Benson rushes to the pharmacist's aid. But then drugs
go missing, and Steph's reputation is at stake. Will Hal risk
his future to save hers?

DEADLY HOMECOMING by Barbara Phinney

All of Northwind Island believes Peta Donald murdered
her ex-boyfriend. No one thinks she's innocent except
newcomer Lawson Mills. And since no one's looking for
the real killer, only *they* can find the truth—before
the killer acts again.

LISCNM1108